WIT

MW00737689

Olive is a story of human endurance spanning four generations from the end of the nineteenth century through to WWII during the almost total destruction of Southampton, a port city in southern England.

Olive is the spine of this historical novel. Ostracised at birth by her family, Olive's life is that of an opportunist and black marketeer. She uses her sex, guile and music skills to move up, but there is a price to be paid and the children bear the cost.

Olive demonstrates the impact one woman had on those whose lives she touched.

Dedication

In remembrance of my mother who offered her support and shared insight and knowledge of the war years, while giving me the opportunity to learn a little about her 'inner self'.

Mum may you have found the peace you so richly deserve.

(Forgiveness comes to those who open their hearts and arms to embrace it.)

Linden Carroll

OLIVE

AUSTIN MACAULEY PUBLISHERS™
LONDON • CAMBRIDGE • NEW YORK • SHARJAH

A CIP catalogue record for this title is available from the British Library.

ISBN 9781786932891 (Paperback)
ISBN 9781786932907 (Hardback)
ISBN 9781786932914 (E-Book)
www.austinmacauley.com

First Published (2017)
Austin Macauley Publishers Ltd.
25 Canada Square
Canary Wharf
London
E14 5LQ

Prologue

This is a story of human endurance spanning WW1 and WW2.

It depicts the spirit and soul of a city in the South of England whose residents, while contributing to the war effort, suffered immeasurable hardships and the devastating, almost total destruction of their beautiful city.

Spanning four generations, it demonstrates the impact one woman had on those whose lives she touched.

A historical novel based in part on fact. Any resemblance to the characters by persons living or dead is purely coincidental.

Chapter 1

The birth

Tears fell and gently washed the newborn's cheek. Martha closed her eyes and steeled herself against the inevitable. They would be coming soon to take her baby away and Martha knew the grievous loss would shadow the rest of her life. Her one request had been that the baby be named Olive, reminiscent of her lineage and warmer climes where the sweet olives grow.

She opened her eyes and looked hard at her daughter, committing to memory the perfect oval face of olive complexion, framed by thick black hair. Large dark lustrous eyes gazed up at her, amazingly focussed for one so young. The babe's gaze held steady, as if she too had a sense of foreboding. Martha marvelled at the infant's features and how like her father she was and thoughts of him invaded her brain. She held her baby tightly and overtaken with emotion, allowed herself once again to indulge in bittersweet memories. How she had loved him then and still…

****

Martha was the last of nine children. Her family was poor and life was a daily grinding battle against the hardship of poverty. It was inconceivable to Martha how she would have survived without Lyza. Her elder sister was the backbone of the family, always watching out for her siblings, ever at hand to listen when her younger sister had a problem. It was always Lyza that Martha would run to, not her mother who was remote and unapproachable. As Martha grew she could see what Lyza's life had become and, fully cognizant of her sister's future, vowed to take the first offer of marriage she received from any prospective husband just to get away from the whole miserable scene. When Bert had come into Martha's life, she saw a way out and gladly entered into the relationship, thinking her life would change for the better.

What a good-looking man Bert was and certainly turned it to his advantage with the women. Even though Martha worked all day in the tavern she looked forward to joining Bert in the lounge bar in the evening. His flirting, cheeky wink and engaging smile won her over completely and when he had asked her out on a date she readily accepted welcoming his attention with open arms. She would spend endless time making herself attractive and appealing and loved the way her neighbours stole approving glances at the two of them. Bert would always find a quiet romantic table away from the bar and their evenings were filled with laughter. Bert's jokes, although a little raw, were funny.

Sometimes they would take a day trip to the beach. They could see the Isle of Wight off in the distance. Martha particularly liked those outings. The sea never really warmed up at any time of the year; a little cold for swimming, but wonderful to walk arm in arm at the water's edge. Their happiness was marred only by the times when Bert would sink into some kind of space where she was obviously not welcome. Martha wondered what caused these mood changes and at the onset realized their day was finished. Isolating himself in his own world, Bert was unreachable; conversation ceased and he would usually blurt out some excuse to end their time together. Martha, although hurt, would always make allowances for his shortcomings.

They had been married only a short while when the bitter truth began to emerge and Martha realized, too late, what a horrendous mistake she had made. Bert's mood changes were hard to bear. Days would pass and he barely spoke. Martha would be consumed with guilt as to whether she had hurt him in some way but in between these bouts, he was wonderfully attentive to her needs and she wondered why she ever doubted his intentions. His behaviour, however, became more and more unpredictable and the marriage rapidly took a downhill slide.

Martha was reduced to servitude, nothing but a skivvy, a chattel to treat how her husband saw fit. Crude and periodic advances on her were usually generated by a stomach full of beer and Bert's violence overwhelming knowing she couldn't reciprocate. Arguing, or showing any sign of her disgust, simply incurred more wrath. She withdrew from him and the world in general, becoming a shadow of her former self.

Late again, following yet another absence from work, she hurled herself through the back door of the tavern and was frantically dragging the strings of her apron around her when her manager appeared in the change room.

"I'd like a word with you," he called over his shoulder on his way to his office, "and don't bother putting on that apron, you'll not be needing it."

Martha knew what was coming; she'd missed work so many times, not wishing her workmates or worse her boss to see the bruises on her body. The worst injuries were always hidden. Bert, in common with other abusers, was very conscious of where he delivered his fists.

"Sorry, luv, got to let you go, I simply can't afford to run a charity here. The patrons are complaining of poor service and the other girls are fed up with being overworked covering your shifts. I've turned a blind eye as long as I can."

Hardly aware of his voice in the background, Martha's brain raced ahead trying to determine how she was going to make up for the loss of income. Hanging up her apron on her way out, she was gratified when her boss pushed a few notes into her hand saying, "You take care of yourself and sorry things didn't work out."

Work was scarce, but she did finally manage to get some simple alteration jobs and took in laundry; but as fast as she earned a few pounds, Bert was waiting on it and relieved her of the money, forcibly if it was not handed over voluntarily; very little in the way of food found its way to the pantry. The bartender at the tavern, however, was always pleased to see Bert.

****

It was early in the year and the air was crisp. She had made her deliveries and picked up several jobs for the next day or so. The weight of the bags was slowing her down but her heart was light as she made her way through the water meadows. She paused to rest a while at her favourite spot close to the river where two streams of crystal clear water gurgled through the reeds, becoming one as they leapt into the fast flowing current. Her fascination had heightened after reading an article about the river named the Itchen. Reading material was always scarce and she was gratified when she occasionally managed to get hold of the daily newspaper and the latest news and information.

She could imagine the river further east of Winchester, gathering momentum, channelled now by the force of several different streams running precariously close to the great Winchester Cathedral. Deemed to be one of the finest chalk streams in England, it ran over multi-coloured pebbles lying on a bed of chalk, rushing south through the shimmering green, lush water meadows of Hampshire. The air was alive with the sounds of the birds and in summer heavy with the scent of phlox. Martha would follow the river up to where several rivulets joined the Itchen, fast running beautiful clear streams. She would fling herself down in the sweet smelling grass; the sun warming her body, renewing her spirit and soul. This early in the year; however, there was a chill in the air. Stately sage green reeds lined the banks of the river competing for space with the cuckoo pint or "skunk cabbage" with bright yellow body swaddled in green cloak. Martha noted with delight that the cuckooflower or lady's smock cowslip was just beginning to poke through the soft grasses and recalled one poem of the few which she'd learnt at school:

When daisies pied and violets blue

And lady's smocks all silver-white

And cuckoo buds of yellow hue

Do paint the meadows with delight.

(W. Shakespeare)

How she would have loved to study the great works of Shakespeare and other poets but the opportunity was never available for her.

Martha watched the Itchen's current picking up, rushing on course impatient to meet with its sister the River Test, forging forward, becoming a raging torrent, until both joined and hurtled hand in hand down to the sea. The water looked so inviting. All she had to do was to step off the bank and be swept away into oblivion. She could almost feel herself sinking into the darkness, the weeds drawing her ever closer to her infinity.

Suddenly, aware that she was not alone, she turned and found herself looking into the darkest, deepest eyes. Unable to avert her gaze, she was drawn inexplicably to the man. Leaping to her feet without a backward glance she ran until she reached home. Her cheeks were burning as she hurled herself up her garden path. Once inside the house, she leaned against the bathroom wall, a cold wet cloth to her face soothing her enflamed skin. Unable to fathom her feelings, the power and magnetism of the dark stranger still held her in unrelenting grasp.

Some days later, having picked up some more dressmaking jobs from the village, Martha took her usual turn off through the water meadows and sat by the streams rushing into her beloved river. Losing track of time, once again the river swathed her in its magic but she was instantly aware of his presence as he sat down close to her. An aura of unspoken calm engulfed them. He reached for her hand as she was about to leave. Her own familiarity amazed her when spontaneously she, too, held his hand tightly as if to stop herself falling back into that black pit which had become her life. It was as if she had stepped over the threshold into another world, a world of caring, loving and mutual respect.

Their secret meetings became her lifeline. The moment they parted, she felt the dull ache of loneliness and despair. She lived for the next time they were able to steal a few minutes together. When he held her in his arms she was lost to him, totally and completely, oblivious even to the sounds of her beloved river. Wrapped in his embrace she could smell the salt in his skin, hear only his soft lilting voice. Sometimes he would sing his gypsy songs, full of the souls of ancient people from ancient times, his heritage from the Ganges through Europe to this tiny island. Other times he would speak of his culture, travels, his people, their dance and the music, then with haunted expression, he spoke of persecution, racialism and hardship and she would hold him closely with all the strength of her being.

Their love was all consuming. When they were together, past and present became one and merged into oblivion becoming one joyous moment, the ‘here and now’. Their shared moments became the mainstay of her existence; to be cherished and brought out of her treasure chest once in a while, to be held and then gently put away lest too much remembrance weaken her, rendering her incapable of handling the life that had become her ‘here and now’.

****

Ripped back to the present, Martha buried her face in the warm little body she held so tightly, her thoughts racing. Oh God what have we done?

Chapter 2

Bert

Bert tidied up the humble room, threw a few cushions on the sofa and straightened the lace runners. He wiped the sweat off his brow with the back of his sleeve feeling the strain of exertion. Since he had been out of work his unhealthy physical state had worsened and he certainly wasn't used to doing anything around the house which he considered most definitely 'women's work.'

****

Bert was a man with no formal training or education and took whatever work he could find, usually as a labourer working in the docks and commonly referred to as a 'dockcc' unloading and loading ships upon their arrival or departure. Classed as casual work, the men would have to line up for work on the new vessels in port. Only a chosen few were lucky; the rest were passed over until the next time when the whole process repeated.

When he had been lucky and been given a few hours or days of work, Bert found it hard and every ounce of his endurance was tested, but even though the pay was poor, he was glad to get it. There were no set working conditions and although unions were legalized in the 1870s before Bert's working time, there was still no provision to improve the lot of unskilled workers until the 1880s when more unions formed focussing on improving conditions both for unskilled workers and also women in the workplace.

The Great London Dock Strike in 1889 crippled the port and many families went hungry, which the employers counted on to drive the strikers back, but they stood their ground and were fully supported by charitable organizations and other Trades Unions, some of which came out in sympathy. Eventually over 150,000 members were involved in the strike which lasted several weeks, causing the busiest port in the world to come to a standstill. Major demands were finally met, setting a precedent in the labour force for the rest of time throughout the country. Huge increases in union membership resulted in improved employment conditions and Bert was now guaranteed a minimum of four hours' work at any one time; his hourly rate for the job increased and being a fully paid up union member, he was offered more jobs.

Yes, things were looking up for Bert and he fell into a bachelor type of life style with his new found wealth, frequenting the taverns far too regularly with the lads. Having an eye for the ladies, he was completely bowled over when he first met Martha; she was so beautiful and he determined to make her his own. She was cleaning tables in the local tavern when he first saw her. He noticed how accomplished she was, her hands moving deftly as she cleaned the tables and set them up for the next customer. Her smile lit up the room and he could see she worked hard for her meagre tips. He was flattered when she accepted his advances without hesitation. Soon they were married and with her few pence a week and his situation vastly improved, they were able to rent a small cottage. They grew a few vegetables and fruit and for a while life seemed to be taking a turn for the better.

Bert had been used to his bachelor life style and all the womanizing it entailed. He wanted it all and yet still come home to a cooked meal and a warm body to cuddle up to in bed. He became complacent in his newfound security and with a bit of money in his pocket, his drinking bouts became more frequent. Gradually work for him became scarcer.

The London and South Western Railway (L&SWR) in operation from the 1830s to 1920s had developed a vast network extending from London to the south of England making commuting a much better proposition. Bert's mate had a little money saved and thinking they could do better working in the London Docks the two boarded a London-bound train in high spirits, jostling each other just like old times when they'd been growing up together. Their joy was short lived, however, soon to turn to disillusionment.

While the two mates were able to land themselves work the going was tough and their travels back south to see their families became more and more infrequent as they were afraid that any missed ship could have been the one that really paid off. The situation became steadily worse with so many hundreds of men looking for work that foremen, known as 'gaffers', once again chose the younger groups who were moved ahead of the line while the older ones such as Bert and his mate were pushed further and further to the end. Money was fast running out.

The railway also ran ships out of Southampton Docks since the 1840s under another shipping name. Gaining power rapidly they were able to buy the Docks by the 90s. The increase in the number of ships coupled with huge development and expansion of the docks persuaded Bert and his mate to return south thinking conditions were ideal for them to get back into the workforce.

Back on home ground, Bert once again entered a deadly cycle of work, drink, then no work and hanging around the union hall and docks waiting for something. On those days when no work came his way, he would arrive home in ill humour, screaming and bullying Martha, once again to the point of physical violence.

****

He threw a pillow down on the sofa in disgust recalling that night…

****

Returning home from the union hall he found Martha sleeping. He remembered his blind rage as he shook her viciously. Perhaps he shouldn't have been so rough with her but it was her own fault. She deserved it he thought, no dinner prepared and her sleeping while he was out looking for work. What the devil was she thinking? She'd started bawling trying to push him away. It was then that he'd noticed her thickened midriff.

"I 'ope you're not in the family way," he raged.

Unable to speak, Martha hung her head and sobbed.

“Answer me woman, when I ask you a question.”

She nodded, still unable to speak.

“How far along are you?”

“The midwife said about four months,” she replied meekly. “The baby will be born in the autumn.”

Trying to be a little more compassionate, he reached for her, but she had leapt to her feet and rushed from the room.

It was later when they were eating he noticed she averted her gaze and suddenly the realization overcame him.

“You whore,” he yelled. “It ain’t my kid is it? I was away in London.”

She looked at him mesmerised in terror.

He brought his fist down on her so hard it knocked her out of the chair.

****

“Out of work again, and now this,” he muttered savagely, hurling another cushion across the room. “How could she have betrayed me like this? Messing around with another bloke and us hardly married. Serve her right if I threw her out in the gutter where she belongs," he ranted. I'll give the brat my name, but that's all it'll get from me. No point in spreading our dirty linen around and the sooner it's on its way the better. There'll be no other bloke's offspring in my house."

He thought of Lyza momentarily. Much as he loathed her, what a blessing it was that she'd stepped in and offered to rear the kid and was far enough away as not to be a hindrance. Thank God for small mercies.

Chapter 3

The adoption

Lyza smoothed her skirts and velvet jacket and hurried across the thickly carpeted floor. She pulled the heavy drapes over the net curtains to keep the sun from fading the silk lampshades, each one hand-made and edged with tassels, so popular at the time.

Her home, a large Victorian house, was set on a long narrow lot and although severe, had a certain charm, with intricate lace panels at the casement windows and heavy brocade curtains hung in rich colours. Lace chair-backs and arm protectors adorned the velvet furniture, heavily embellished with buttons and fringes. Most of the rooms had been unused for years and dust cloths covered their exquisite antique furnishings. Once in a while the coverings were removed for laundering and carefully replaced.

Lyza went and checked out the nursery to make sure that everything was in order and prepared ready for her new arrival; crib, clean towels, cloth diapers, etc. Who would ever have imagined that I would be rearing a child at my age? She asked herself. Of her own volition she had accepted the impending task and feeling somewhat overwhelmed, sat down hard in the old rocking chair to brace herself for the upcoming meeting. That she was prepared to take her sister's infant under her wing and rear her as her own should not have been daunting as her altruistic lifestyle of doing for others and neglecting her own needs personified her very existence.

****

Lyza's early childhood had been fairly happy. She had enjoyed the benefits of being an only child in the early days, but with each successive arrival of a new brother or sister, times became increasingly tough and Lyza's mother began to rely on the young girl completely. Her beloved music and reading was pushed further into the background as she was required to handle all the dressmaking and mending repairs, along with the laundry for the rest of the children. Her one joy was when she was invited to her Cousin Jeremy's house for afternoon tea and she was allowed to visit the expansive library at the back of the house which overlooked the beautiful Victorian garden. She took advantage of every possible moment to expand her knowledge, lovingly dusting off the books with a long handled feather duster then sitting avidly devouring the pages of her latest choice.

She loved to open the huge French doors and wander down the garden, a magical place where dreams were spun and hope and inspiration abounded, promoting peace and creating an ambiance conducive to quiet study and contemplation. A majestic red brick wall surrounded the garden on which brightly coloured Red Admiral butterflies basked in the warm summer sun, lazily flexing their wings; their stark red and black colours so sharply defined they seemed a little contrived. Each succeeding generation of robins sat on top of the wall surveying their domain swelling their little red breasts filling the garden with song. Antirrhinum (snapdragons) showed their faces in the summer through every little crack in the stonework where the birds had carried the seeds. They were of all colours and when both sides were squeezed they opened up like the mouths of tiny rabbits; hence the nickname ‘bunny rabbits’. The nickname had been around as long as Lyza could remember and she wondered who had first assigned it so appropriately to these blooms.

Oversized bumble bees in their yellow and black striped furry shirts would wallow in the warmth of the paved garden path which ran the length of the garden.

They were largely responsible for the propagation of the beautiful Tradescantia, a gorgeous blue to violet coloured flower set in sage green reed like leaves. Lyza had read that this beautiful plant was said to have been named after John Tradescantia, the gardener of Charles 1 in 1638 and grew in abundance in the garden. It was also interesting to note that the flowers opened on overcast days but closed when confronted with sharp direct sunlight. All of these themes were captured and replicated in her delicate watercolours and woven into her intricate embroidery.

****

Lyza had remained with her family, who moved constantly to different rented homes in the quest to find cheaper accommodation. After her sister had married and left to embark on her new life, seemingly full of promise, Lyza devoted herself to the care and nurturing of her mother and siblings, thus forfeiting any hope of a family of her own.

One day Jeremy invited her over for afternoon tea and greeting her warmly guided her into the parlour. When they were comfortably settled, he leaned forward and looked at her sharply,

"Lyza my dear, you really should give a thought to your own life now. You've done more than your share. Now that most of your siblings have gone their own way, you should look to your own needs. I've received an offer to go to the United States to build up the family law company and am looking to rent out this house. I would like to offer it to you as your home in exchange for housekeeping services. As you know I have many valuable antiques and furnishings and would much prefer to have someone I can trust as a caretaker. For those services I would be prepared to offer the accommodation for a very nominal rent which would be negotiable, as I'm more interested in having the old house cared for properly and you would be at liberty to sublet a room or two. I, of course, would have to vet any tenants and review their references, etc. Now, Lyza, what do you say?"

"Jeremy, I don't know what to say. I'm absolutely overwhelmed at your generosity; do you really think I could manage?"

"Of course you could and remember I'll be in the background to back you up." He chortled and, feeling very proud of himself, grabbed her hand. "So that settles that then, now let's have some tea."

****

Lyza rocked gently backwards and forwards enjoying the comfort of the old chair. The house would definitely be an ideal setting for a growing child with a beautiful garden to play in and a wonderful library and piano to develop all sorts of cultural activities. Yes she would grow up as a 'lady'. Thank goodness for Jeremy's kindness in giving both of them the chance to live in this beautiful old house. Knowing she would have to generate some kind of income, Lyza wondered how she would go about it. She was an excellent seamstress and had also taught music and the piano to the odd child over the years. A lucrative business could be built up providing services specifically for the more 'well to do' clients. There were a number of financially privileged folks around and some of the mothers would be glad to have their children benefit from a musical background. What with that and providing some good dressmaking services, she should be able to manage. Her thoughts ran rampant as she laid her plans. She'd need to get organized with professional business cards advertising her services.

Lyza had been eking out a living by taking in students for music lessons and sewing jobs around the neighbourhood. The years had been hard for her, scrimping and scraping to save a few pennies here and there. Women were expected to marry at an early age because there was very little opportunity for them to succeed in the workforce. Even though the trades unions were becoming more organized with unskilled and women workers becoming unionized, the memberships were still predominately for thc engineering trades.

"I'll get in touch with Jeremy as soon as I find a suitable tenant and give him all the particulars. A lodger would certainly generate extra income and I could even provide meals, if required and laundry services," she said excitedly reinforcing her plans.

Her thoughts turned again to her beloved sister, Martha, who had married at the first opportunity. Lyza had taken an instant dislike to Bert, the new husband and the feeling was reciprocated. Bert viewed Lyza with contempt, knowing that, although poor, she was a station above him. She was well read, knowledgeable, with a quiet courteous manner and he felt out of his depth and uncomfortable around her, only too well aware of his own inadequacies, which made him even more defensive.

When she had been told of her sister's indiscretion, to avert the wrath of Martha's coarse husband Bert, who would have surely thrown both mother and child out on the street to fend for themselves, Lyza had offered to raise the child. Her mother ungraciously offered to assume the responsibility but upon reflection, the family decided they didn't want the baby and Lyza's offer to rear the child until she was of age, as her adoptive parent, was readily accepted.

Martha had been confined to the local midwife's accommodation, as Bert had made it quite clear that she was not having the baby in his house, although it was general practice for women to give birth in their own homes. The midwife, named Gertrude, was a strict but generally caring person and Lyza had paid her well to make sure her sister received the care she needed.

A meeting had been scheduled at Gertrude's house for all parties concerned to execute informal adoption paperwork.

****

"Right then," said Lyza decisively, giving herself false courage, "the sooner we get this over with the better." She stood up and moved towards the long, severe mirror bordering the dark hallway and carefully placed her hat on her head firmly pushing the pins in place. One more smooth of her skirts, a check of the laces on her boots and she made her way out. Had she forgotten anything? She picked up her purse and was now beginning to feel the strain. The pressure was building and her heart was pounding. A liaison with Bert was more than she could handle, but handle it she would. Nothing must go wrong with the transfer. She took a firm hold of the elaborate pram with its huge wheels and leather panelling. Having practised pushing it around the garden, Lyza now considered herself an expert.

****

Lyza arrived promptly for her appointment. Gertrude's home was a quaint little cottage with thatched roof, although small, was more than adequate for the needs of many young women, cast out for one reason or another when they were pregnant. Bert was waiting by the porch when she arrived. The two merely nodded at one another, both aware of the mutual dislike each had for the other. An old tabby cat sat sunning under the porch eyeing them suspiciously. Bert glared at it fleetingly and then turned his attention to Lyza.

"Well let's get on with it, I haven't got all day," he mouthed sullenly.

Gertrude opened the door. She appeared to be everything she should be. A short but strongly made woman of stocky build. Her white hair sharply drawn back giving her a look of severity but she was obviously a kind and very capable woman. She ushered them into a tiny parlour where she had prepared tea and scones. Lyza noted, although a humble dwelling, Gertrude did everything in a very proper manner and the tray was beautifully laid, with lace doilies in the saucers and delicate napkins at the ready. Fresh homemade jam and butter accompanied a most appetizing array of scones, also placed on a lace mat.

The local vicar, already in attendance, was nervously arranging a scone when they entered the room. Given the circumstances, Bert and Lyza made themselves as comfortable as possible and drank their tea in silence. Suddenly there was a loud wrapping on the door and Gertrude went to let in the last participant, Herbert, the family's barrister. Herbert was a close friend of Cousin Jeremy, as his company handled the British side of Jeremy's business dealings while he conducted his other affairs in the States. Herbert had offered to witness the documents authorizing Lyza to rear the girl and to provide her with all her necessities until she was of age and would be meeting with Lyza and her charge at intervals to assess and review progress.

Gertrude showed Herbert into the room and then excused herself from the uncomfortable group and abysmal circumstances. She was going to prepare Martha and the baby in the occasional room at the back of the house. The vicar followed her as she entered the little room to prepare himself for the christening. Herbert had accompanied Martha and Bert a few days previously to register the baby's birth and she had been formally named Olive. To everyone's amazement, Bert had allowed his name to be entered in the registry as the father of the child.

Lyza discussed a few intricacies regarding the documentation with Herbert and after what seemed an interminable period of time Gertrude appeared and summoned them all to the occasional room.

The ceremony went very smoothly. The baby slept soundly on the vicar's arm while he dabbed his 'holy water' on her forehead. The business then concluded and Lyza was relieved to see that out of respect to Martha, the vicar gently handed the infant to her mother for placement in the pram. Lyza's heart went out to her sister whose face was set in stone, a ghastly grey pallor.

Herbert directed them all to the table and produced a pen for each to sign. He instructed them on the legalities and provisos. After the signing, Gertrude wheeled the sleeping child out followed closely by the group with the exception of Lyza who wanted a quiet moment with Martha.

"Martha, dear," she spoke softly to her sister. "Whenever you are able to sneak away, I want you to know you are always welcome to come to my house and visit us any time."

She saw a flicker of light in the young girl's eyes as she bowed her head, so overcome with unutterable grief and sobbing, she could hardly support her own frail body.

"Remember, dear, there is always an open door whenever you can get away," Lyza reiterated striving for control of her emotions. She hugged the girl briefly not wishing to prolong the misery and departed in haste.

Fortunately and to her immense relief, Bert had already left. The vicar muttered some felicitations, donned his hat primly and also made a hasty exit.

"Now, Lyza, we will meet bi-monthly initially. Here's the schedule I've set up; the first Monday on alternate months." Herbert spoke briskly. "I'll drop by your house from the office, at 6:00 p.m. Oh! About your prospective tenants, I'll handle all that for you on behalf of Jeremy, just keep me in the picture." He shook hands with Lyza and Gertrude and left.

Gertrude was busily stuffing the last of the baby's personal goods into the pram. "Lyza, I'll expect to see you each week with the babe so that I can check her out. What would be a good time for you?"

"Oh I think Monday morning would be good, as I will be meeting with Herbert on Mondays every couple of months. I'll have both reports to you and Herbert; keep it tidy."

"Very well then, I'll see you both out," said Gertrude hurrying ahead to the make sure the passage was clear for them all.

Lyza pushed the pram down the path, pausing to look back. The cat was gazing into space, probably thinking of the next helpless little creature it would drag in, she thought, and drop its remains onto the faded tapestry rug; a nice little offering for Gertrude to dispose of. She promptly forgot the cat and gazing upwards knew she would carry with her forever the vision of Martha at the window. Lyza had rarely seen such desolation in a person's face, particularly one so young. Her sister turned away, shoulders convulsing with her uncontrollable weeping. Lyza also turned and set her path for home.

"I have a child to rear now so I'd better stay focussed and in control and keep a tight rein on myself," she muttered under her breath, fighting to stay on top of her emotions. "This definitely isn't the time to get distracted and swayed off course."

Chapter 4

Romany times

The little boy sat on the shaft of the red and yellow caravan. A handsome lad with olive complexion and hair as black as the crow perched on the neighbouring shaft. They were part of the gypsy encampment gathered in the woodland glade. The caravans were hand painted with multi-coloured wooden panels and scalloped eaves. The horses that pulled them were grouped a short distance away, avidly munching on the fresh green shoots growing on the sunny perimeter of the glade. Their tack still in place on their gleaming bodies, harnesses and saddles elaborately etched with designs of Roma culture. Their manes were adorned with ribbons tied lovingly by the gypsy women, who decorated their own flowing hair in the same manner.

The boy laughed and clucked at the crow, who hopped boldly up the shaft, his beady little eyes bright in anticipation of a hand-out. The boy, instead, reached for his lyre and picked at the cords.

Some of the women were milling around gathering wood for the evening fire; their long skirts multi-coloured, reflecting the bright tones of the caravans; others were preparing vegetables. They worked fast, their fingers nimbly scraping and chopping and dropping their preparations into the cauldrons to go on the fire. The men smoothed and oiled the wheel axles on the vans, stopping for a smoke at regular intervals and falling into deep discussion about their next stopping point.

Roman was to remember these times throughout his life.

The routine was much the same: travel through the days; set up camp at night. Sometimes, depending on the season, the travellers would stay longer in some areas. They took what work was available; the farmers expecting them and glad of their cheap labour, reserved fields on their land for their visitors to set up camp. The Roma were exploited but happy with the simplicity of working the land and grateful to receive the miserable pittance metered out to them. When they were not working the land, they carved wooden clothes pegs and moved around the community sharpening knives and other implements. Their women went door to door selling the pegs, flower posies with ribbon rosettes, and were also adept at telling fortunes for the more inquisitive consumers.

Berry season was always welcome; apart from the wonderful pies, Roman's mouth watered at the thought of the light golden crust, covering a melange of sweet fruit. The pies were also a source of income placed carefully in the baskets woven by the women and sold door to door.

It seemed an idyllic life, but, as Roman approached manhood, he became more aware of the downside of the living and the issues and problems that had to be dealt with day by day.

Sometimes, if Roman was inclined, he would retrieve his horse from the makeshift corral, pack his saddle bags and head out on a three or four-day mental therapy 'ride around' as he called it. His horse, a traditional Gypsy Cob, was multi-coloured and beautifully marked with flowing mane and tail and stamina, well able to handle much longer trips than Roman's little expeditions. Her loving, trusting nature, typical of her breed, made her a loyal companion. Roman suspected she enjoyed her 'retreats' as much as himself.

Their trips would generally follow the river to where it joined the Test at its estuary in Southampton Water when they were in Hampshire. On occasion Roman would ride the entire length, in excess of 28 miles, passing through the Itchen Valley en route. The eating was good with watercress in abundance, growing only in the purest of water and an ample supply of resident fish, such as snipe, brook lamprey, Atlantic salmon, Roman's favourite being the wild brown and rainbow trout which were superb. He always had a wonderful sense of contentment and well-being on these excursions which remained with him for quite some time following his return to camp.

****

His mother had named him Roman her favourite name and because she likened it to the gypsy word Rom meaning man, and the language he would learn being Romany, closely related to Sanskrit, one of the oldest Indo-European languages of the ancient Hindus of India, the birth of the gypsy heritage.

Roman soon learned it was not just his skin tone and features that set him apart but also the gypsies' itinerant life style, indicative of their culture. Their individualism set the Roma apart; they didn't fit into any of the various societal groups. The difference caused them to be feared and scorned, subjected to racism and persecution and classed as thieves and marauders. Their only sin being that they wanted to live a free life, earn only what they needed to sustain themselves and live in the close family network of warmth, security in love, music and dance. Their animals, too, were loved and firmly ensconced in the family structure.

Music and dance were the essence of the gypsies; without these their life force would weaken and die. At sunset the camp was set up and the group would gather round the fire having eaten a hearty dinner. The music and dance would begin. Songs would tell of their ancestors' migration west, their persecution and even slavery. Their instruments, the violin in particular echoed the deep melancholy of the moment. Many instruments would be heard; the accordion, lyre, guitar and all were similar to those found in Russia, Hungary and Greece, countries the travellers had passed through over the centuries. Their musical diversity rendered their sounds unique even with undertones of the bagpipes and because they were such gifted musicians, their music was accepted worldwide, even when they themselves were not. Such was the contrary nature of humans.

Roman became a gifted musician. He would play his violin and move his audience to tears and to the depths of despair and then raise them up to the pinnacles of joy. The young men and women would be caught up in the romantic and even licentious undertones as they danced, and the momentum increased and the flesh of young and old grew hot and the dancing reached a frenzy to the point of madness; and the night grew old and weak as did the desire, except to sleep. Such was the life.

****

He was drawn inexplicably to her from the first time he saw her. It was an inevitable crossing of paths, the crossroads of their lives. Paths each had walked every day growing ever closer to each other. Their meeting was the culmination of their very existence – everything else inconsequential.

He had seen her on many occasions by the river, watching her closely as she approached, smiling as she threw herself down on the grassy riverbank, revelling in the cool fragrance of the lush reeds. He likened her to a young wild animal stretching and luxuriating seemingly full of the pure joy of living. Locked in her own space her face wore a soft unguarded look as she gazed about her laughing sometimes at the antics of the field mice, of which there were many or migratory birds such as the Meadow Pipit and Warblers which made the long journey every summer from Africa to nest and raise their families on British terrain.

Their first encounter was totally unexpected to both of them. She was sitting perfectly still, cocooned in the reeds along the riverbank, wrapped up in the music of the river, the flowing and eddying and the dazzling sun touching the very tips of each wave as it rushed to join the many whirlpools of which the river was so famous.

He had been compelled to move closer and leaping to her feet she was gone as if a figment of his imagination. He remained by the river for a long time feeling the heavy weight of desolation on his shoulders. She had touched him so briefly and yet so completely. He wondered if he would ever see her again.

Following that meeting he was overjoyed when he'd seen her again while heading towards the river. She was sitting at her favourite spot, the neck of the two streams coursing through the meadows rushing towards the river. She sat unmoving like a beautiful statue placed amongst the reeds to be admired for all time. Roman sat down quietly beside her and on this occasion, she remained motionless gazing across the water. They were silent for a while and suddenly Martha had once again stood up abruptly. Without thinking he had taken her hand in his and she had willingly held on to him as if she would never let him go. Neither comprehended the magnitude of their feelings but both knew they were entering a vortex from which there was no escape.

"I must go, I'll be missed and it will just make things worse for me. Please forgive me for being so familiar, you just caught me at a bad time. Thank you for the comfort, but I really must go."

Roman's voice was harsh with strain. "Will I see you again?"

"I come to the river as often as I can, it's the only place I can get peace and feel some level of contentment. I can't arrange to meet you, that wouldn't be right, but as I say, I come here whenever I get a few minutes," she said rushing off before she had a chance to change her mind.

Following that day, they snatched their moments whenever possible. The two would sit motionless. Sometimes Martha would break their silence with an excited cry, "Oh look, a meadow pipit, see the lovely soft yellow under feathers speckled with dark brown spots. See it's gathering twigs to build a nest. Did you know one of the best places to find a cuckoo's egg is in a meadow pipit's nest? You'd wonder why they build their nests on the ground, making it easy for the larger bird to knock out one of the eggs and lay its own." She always delighted in the rustling of the reeds, softly whispering. "Watch carefully, the reed warblers have arrived. You have to look very closely they spend their time climbing amongst the reeds in the water as they fly only short distances. You'll have to wade out in the shallows if you want to see their nests.

"Hold your horses," Roman would laughingly say, "you're going a mile a minute. I can't digest all this information in one sitting."

Still she launched on, ignoring the interruption.

"The sedge warblers are much more colourful with a black stripe over their eyes; they prefer to nest in the sedges instead of the reeds. If you listen you'll hear their beautiful song, it's much louder than the reed warbler. Hard to believe they're cousins, they are so completely different."

Roman, already an authority on wildlife, would smile as Martha would get more and more technical. He had to admit she was certainly a font of information and he soon became even more familiar with the many feathered visitors abounding the river.

Martha's face was before Roman wherever he went, whatever he did. His thoughts never strayed far from her. When he was with her he was at peace, she was his destiny and he loved and adored her.

Following one such meeting, he returned to the gypsy encampment. His father came towards him and they walked together in companionable silence until his father ventured, "Roman do you think it's wise getting involved with this woman? No good can come of your liaison. There are many young, strong women of our culture available to you."

"I'll have none of them," Roman answered defiantly. "I am lost to her. I want no other, now or ever."

Roman had always been close to his father, but knowing there would be no coming together on this issue he moved away swiftly not wishing to resume the conversation. “I’ll start oiling the rigs,” he said and hurried off in the direction of the vans.

His father shook his head sadly and sighed deeply. “Yes, we’d better start packing up. The farms in Kent are waiting for us. The crops have been good this year, should make up for our losses of last year.”

Usually they left in early spring but had delayed their departure this year as the season had been slow getting under way. He was glad they were moving out, he thought it would be a good break in the routine and maybe Roman would see things differently and come to his senses when they returned to Hampshire to settle in for the winter. He loved his son and wanted the best for him.

A crisp sunny day hailed the next morning which did nothing to dispel Roman’s low spirits as he hitched up the horses ready for the day’s travel.

The journey to Kent would take them several days as they made numerous stops along the way. They would assist other groups within their culture who earned their living by operating fair grounds as entertainers, herbalists and salesmen of collectibles of all descriptions. Roman’s group would help out in the setting up of the stands, tents and displays. Friends and relatives wintered in the Thames marshes, always a popular stopping place and feasting and music following the reunion.

They arrived in Kent in time to begin harvesting the soft fruit and vegetable crops of summer, followed by peas and beans. The hard fruits and vegetable season started in September with the harvesting of hops followed by apples and pears. Potatoes were dug at the onset of winter.

Although the main groups settled around South East London where they had camped traditionally for hundreds of years, Roman's people generally headed back to the New Forest for the winter months. The New Forest offered a place of private, sheltered living with fresh spring water, herbs and an abundance of small game and they always lived very well through to the spring again.

Following his return to Hampshire, at the first opportunity he headed for the river. Sure enough there was Martha. Stopping abruptly in his tracks he was shocked at her desolate, drawn expression, dull, lifeless eyes set in the palest face he had ever seen. Recovering himself he rushed toward her with arms outstretched, but she turned away from him quietly weeping. Finally able to speak, Martha told him of the impending birth and in barely a whisper, "Roman, my sweet love, we've lived our moments and now we have to part." Rising unsteadily to her feet, refusing his hand of assistance she said goodbye to her lover.

Roman sat alone by the river and hung his head in shame, scalding tears burning his eyes.

“Dear God forgive me for the wrong I’ve done this woman. She was life itself to me and gave me my everything just as I took away her everything. Forgive me and watch over her. My sweet Martha, I’ll carry you forever with me my darling and will the time away until we meet again now or hereafter.”

Surging and wailing over the meadows, the wind swallowed his anguished pleadings and disgorged them into oblivion.

Chapter 5

Titanic

Lyza arranged her cushions on the little bench by the wall. This was her favourite spot in the garden, a sheltered little alcove protected by the wind. Olive was at music practice with the school's music teacher, Ms. Brookshields. She had been Lyza's 'project' since her informal adoption by her aunt. Lyza had been determined that no effort would be spared in the further development of any talent or skill the girl possessed.

Ms. Brookshields was a nice woman who promoted any pupil with exceptional voice and music skills. She would manoeuvre each child into the appropriate channels giving them every developmental opportunity. Olive was one such student exhibiting outstanding abilities as a soprano along with her piano skills. Noteworthy also were her amazing mathematical applications; being able to calculate highly advanced equations in her head without once putting pen to paper, far above what was deemed normal even for an adult; furthermore, it was extremely rare for anybody to be so adept in the arts and mathematical areas. Students were usually good at one or the other but not both. Ms. Brookshields wanted her trained as a classical musician, either diverting into opera or the piano, although she recognized her competence in the accounting area. She was obviously brilliant enough to enter any of those fields.

Lyza had experienced great financial difficulty over the past years and realizing Olive's full potential was becoming more and more difficult to achieve, particularly in view of the fact that the girl was wayward and proving difficult to manage. She was wild and did things her own way. Classes were missed and she would disappear for long periods of time.

She had a dark side, so dark as to be frightening. Sometimes the child would look at her aunt with what seemed pure hatred and Lyza would shudder when she recalled such looks. Other times the little girl would drop what she was doing and run to Lyza, throw her arms around her neck and say "Auntie, you know I love you, don't you?" almost as if she were trying to convince herself, as well as her aunt. The girl's duplicitous brain had Lyza filled with confusion, she never knew what to expect.

Olive's stories, while entertaining in any other circumstance, were woven webs of deceit, so elaborate it was difficult to determine which was truth or fiction. Her "make-believe" was so detailed and believable when she relayed certain situations that it never failed to come as a shock when all proved to be a figment of her imagination, how she construed a given incident or just out and out plain lying. The incidents of stealing had been difficult to accept and later to cover up.

Lyza was receiving suspicious looks whenever she went to the school, unspoken words, just looks. The principal had brought up a couple of incidents which made Olive look suspiciously guilty of stealing but nothing was ever conclusive. Lyza was a church going person; it was unthinkable for her that somebody would take something that didn't belong to them. The frustration and helplessness she felt was overwhelming whenever an item or money went missing and the only common factor was that Olive had been in the vicinity. Nothing was ever found in her possession, with the exception of that one horrendous occasion…

Lyza recalled with horror the "party".

The parents of one of the girls had thrown a huge birthday party for their daughter and all the 'specially gifted' in the musical group were invited to go. Lyza was ecstatic when Olive received an invitation, as it was an excellent opportunity for her to fraternize with the 'upper echelon', the class of company which could afford her advancement opportunities in the future. One of the girl's gifts was a gold pendant. Sadly, during the course of the evening, the chain broke and after a display of dramatics and tears worthy of a spoilt, over indulged girl, she tucked the pendant away in her pocket for safekeeping. Much later, it was discovered to be missing. After a thorough search of the premises and children, with the more sensitive wailing hysterically at the injustice served upon them, the search revealed nothing.

Lyza had been to Olive's room to collect the laundry and upon pushing it into the carrying bag, there was a clinking noise. Mesmerised in horror, Lyza found herself gazing at the pendant, hidden amongst the linen. When she had tackled Olive she got the usual elaborate account: "Auntie, how could you accuse me of stealing? How could I possibly do such a thing? I can only think the pendant must have dropped out of her pocket and fallen into hem of my dress. You know how you were always saying the hem needed to be secured but you never got around to it. Well, it's obvious that's how the necklace came to be there." Oh yes, thought Lyza, she always had a way of twisting the truth and putting the onus on somebody else to cover her tracks. How can such a little girl be so devious?

"Olive, I don't care how it came about but I want you to get it back to that girl. You can say you found it or something, anything. I know you'll be able to think of a good answer. You're good at that. Just take it back; I'll have no more of this."

Needless to say, the pendant was never returned and was never seen again. Lyza had gone to lie down. The whole situation was getting out of hand and she no longer knew how to deal with it.

There were some bright moments, though, such as when the fair came to town. One day Olive came rushing into the house yelling, “Auntie, Auntie, the gypsies have come they are setting up their fair in the park, can we go later, can we? Lyza was elated.

“Yes, of course Olive.” That would make a real treat. We’ll hurry with our meal and get down there so as not to miss the fun.”

The gypsies came to town twice a year and set up their fairground wherever they were allowed. Everybody was excited although there were still some that despised them. Their ongoing prejudice manifested itself in fear and subsequent violent behaviour towards the quiet living people. Lyza would take Olive and together they would have a great time. Olive would laugh and chatter and behave just like a normal little girl. Lyza always felt much closer to her on those occasions. She went to her little emergency box of pennies, mustn’t go empty handed she thought, Olive should have a few treats.

When they arrived at the fair ground there were already large numbers of people gathering around the various stalls. Olive, as usual rushed towards the “roll a penny” booth, which was her favourite. Lyza reached in her pocket and gave her two pennies. It was a game of chance. The penny was rolled down a grooved piece of wood and onto a sheet of coloured squares with a black border on each. The figure on the square denoted a cash amount. If the penny landed on a square clear of the black border, the player would receive the cash equivalent. Should it be a winner, more often than not it would be lost again in the fever of trying to land on more squares and earn even more money.

"Look at that," Olive positively screamed, "I've won three pence."

A brown hand moved across the counter and plonked the pennies in the young girl's hand. Olive looked up at the toothless smile she encountered and wondered fleetingly how the man could eat his food. It was only a passing thought; however, as she was bent on winning more money. Lyza, who was standing a little way off cast her eyes around. Why there's that same man again, she thought, she had noticed him the last time they were at the fair and also he had been at the end of the street on occasion.

One day Martha had come to visit and Lyza, drawing the curtains, noticed he was again at the corner. She could not understand why Martha had stopped dead in her tracks when she had seen him and the two had been locked in each other's gaze. It was almost as if the world had stood still and they were the only two people on the planet. He had looked at Martha in the same way as he was looking at the child now, oblivious to everything except the girl. His eyes drank in her every movement as if he never wanted the moment to end. He smiled and the harshness of his dark features softened momentarily. Why, it's almost as if he has deep feelings for her, Lyza thought as her eyes travelled from one to the other. Then with a sudden intake of breath, my goodness, they are so much alike, they could be related. The rich olive skin and the black shiny hair. The realization of the possibility hit her, especially when she remembered Martha who had wrenched her gaze away from the man and ran stumbling up the path. When Lyza had shown her into the parlour and gone to make the tea, she had heard the quiet sobbing. Not wishing to intrude, she made no mention of the subject but noted Martha's poor swollen eyes when she re-appeared with the tea tray.

Tearing herself away from the thought, Lyza shouted across to Olive.

"Come Olive, let's go the coconut sty and see if we can knock a coconut off its stand. They have lots of lovely prices, it's worth a try and after that we can go and get some candy floss."

At the mention of the latter, Olive quickly ran to her aunt.

"Auntie, can we have some candy floss now and then go to the coconut stand?"

“Of course, what a good idea,” Lyza replied, glad to leave the scene, as the man’s gaze had now fastened on her and she felt mildly uncomfortable. The incident was soon forgotten as she and Olive found themselves with candyfloss stuck all over their faces and oh how they laughed, certainly a day to be remembered, both so happy and comfortable with each other. Lyza said a silent prayer of thanks.

****

Stirring herself realizing how late it was, Lyza leapt to her feet and hurried inside. It was a fresh April day and even though she was warmly dressed, sitting outside had chilled her through to the bone. She had made a warm broth and homemade bread for dinner and eagerly went in to prepare it for Olive coming home. I had better pop down to Joe’s in the morning, she thought, as she was going through the cupboards for supplies while preparing dinner. She always shopped for her groceries at the little shop which Joe and his wife Mary ran between them. I wonder if Joe and Mary would like to come for dinner tomorrow night, she mused, I’ll ask them in the morning.

****

It was April 10, 1912 a momentous occasion. Every able body that could get themselves to Southampton dock rushed to see the great transatlantic liner the Titanic take off on her maiden voyage to New York, USA, taking with her over 2,000 passengers and crew. The whole world was following the journey of the biggest ship ever built. Everybody it seemed was talking about the incredible liner, created to carry passengers and operate as a mail service between Southampton and New York. She had been constructed in Belfast, Northern Ireland; a huge project taking three years to complete, bringing employment and putting bread on the table for many poor families; overshadowed by the death of several construction workers who lost their lives because of inadequate facilities to serve such a mammoth project.

"Auntie, we'd better get a move on," said Olive, pushing her feet into her boots. The intricate laces were always a constant source of irritation to her, being always in a hurry to get into some new venture. The two were going to see the great ship off if they got the chance knowing that the crowds would be huge. When they arrived, it was as they suspected with so many people jostling and pushing to get a glimpse of the departure but they managed to squeeze in and get a good view. What an amazing feat of human ingenuity, an unbelievably beautiful, regal ship and she was given a royal send off.

The glory was short-lived, however, and her story was to be told and remembered forever. The great ship never arrived at her destination. Four days into her trip she collided with an iceberg and sank in the early hours of the next morning, killing over 1,500 men, women and children. The whole world was aghast. It was one of the greatest marine tragedies of all time. Notices of the catastrophe were being posted throughout Southampton. The City's horrified silence was broken only by the anguished wailing of women, many with children and babes in arms as they gathered in the streets waiting for word on the casualties, many of whom had family members on the fated ship.

In the days that followed, the whole town remembered and grieved. Lyza went to the church and sat with Joe and Mary. They prayed for those lost who had so eagerly rushed to buy the coveted tickets to be a part of the most affluent passenger list of all time. They prayed for the crew who, at the time of death were so totally ill equipped to carry out their duties and obligations and they prayed for the innocents, those trusting children who never had a chance to live out their lives.

Chapter 6

WW1 begins

The year was 1914, the 4th day of August, a day to be remembered by the citizens of the United Kingdom. Britain declared war on Germany. It was a war to rage throughout the entire world. Even though men rushed to enlist, fired with enthusiastic patriotism; as the war progressed it became clear that more troops were needed. The Government finally introduced subscription. Many thousands never returned to their homes. It was unimaginable that the war would last four long years.

Lyza went to meet with Gertrude for her weekly visit even though Olive was now in her 12th year and no longer required the medical checks as a baby. Both Lyza and Gertrude looked forward to getting together and the tradition was continued. Gertrude was showing her age and the ravages of time were taking their toll, she was nonetheless still a gracious host and after a few preliminaries regarding Olive, would always lead Lyza into the parlour for a pot of tea and cake, usually a scrumptious fruit cake fresh from the oven. Lyza always left with a feeling of well-being. The two had become very close friends over the years and during these troubled times they both derived comfort from their friendship. Lyza had conveyed her fears regarding Olive to Gertrude and both agreed to ride it out and hope it was a phase the child was going through.

"You know, Gertrude, Olive knows she was ousted from the family fold. Her mother tries to see her once in a while but her visits are not well received by Olive. She is very cold towards her and it breaks my heart to see Martha suffer so. Of course Olive is harbouring deep feelings of rejection and maybe this is manifested in her atrocious behaviour. Gertrude, she has always been such a strange child; I never know what she is thinking and her bouts of rage and frustration are frightening. I cringe when there's a knock on the door, I never know if she's been found out and caught stealing or worse."

"Lyza you must stop lashing yourself." Gertrude gesticulated, a habit she had formed when she was anxious and it was impossible for her to keep her hands still, more so when she was constantly repeating herself to Lyza on the subject of Olive. It was becoming tiresome and she privately thought that the girl was a lost cause; she definitely had serious problems. "Surely you know you've done all you can. You spare no effort for the girl. Even though you're on the 'bread line' yourself, you always put her first. What about all her music and singing classes? Look at the concert we just went to, she was called back to the stage many times after her piano session? She's making quite a name for herself with her wonderful talent."

It's not only music she's making a name for herself in, thought Lyza sourly. "Oh well," she said, "we'll just have to tough it out and hope for the best."

Lyza dabbed her mouth with the serviette and folded it neatly on her plate. "Thank you, Gertrude." She touched her friend's hand lightly. "You always make me whole again. I had better get going, I have to go to Joe's and get some provisions. It will only be a few though; the prices are so high now and still climbing. Since the Germans started their U-boat campaign, they're sinking so many of our supply ships nobody can afford the terrible prices because everything is so scarce. Everybody reckons it's a deliberate ploy to starve us out," she said grimly while Gertrude nodded constantly in agreement.

The war had been raging for two long years. During this period people started hoarding provisions to the extent that some shops had actually run out of food. The situation stabilized somewhat but was to become critical again over the next two years.

Lyza stood up abruptly and made her way towards the hallway. Fastening the buttons on her cape she looked into Gertrude's kind sweet face and noted the concern. She put her arms around her friend and hugged her.

"Now Gertrude, please don't start worrying about me, I'll be all right, you know me, I'm a survivor. See you next week, take care."

With that she headed for the door and looking back with a smile and a wave walked quickly down the path on her way to Joe's corner shop.

Joe's had become a bit of an institution. He had started the business from practically nothing selling not only a variety of food supplies but also many other useful items of hardware and household effects. He was always bringing in interesting and practical items and always prepared to barter for the price, although even he was starting to feel the pinch. He was paying so much for his supplies that he had to pass some of the cost on to his patrons. The small bags of coal he had stockpiled were out of reach for some and many people were freezing in their homes but Joe always made sure that the poorest never left the shop without a little extra to see them through.

Two of his sons had rushed to answer the call for volunteers and Joe and Mary his wife, although so proud of their sons, still suffered every day they were gone, agonizing on whether they would ever see them again. They had four other younger children, two of which were young boys for which their mother was eternally grateful. Although much older men enlisted, filled with the need to support the war effort and who should have been turned down, the government did not take little children yet.

Lyza rounded the corner and headed across the road to the shop. It was strangely quiet. As she approached, she was filled with apprehension. To her horror she saw Joe with his head in his hands, tears rolling down his cheeks.

"Joe, whatever is the matter?" she cried.

Joe just shoved the telegram in her hand, "We regret to inform you…" It was little Alfred, the younger of the two sons, wiped out before he even reached full manhood; never had a chance to live.

"Oh my God, how could you let this happen?" she said over and over again.

She laid her hand in comfort on his shoulder. "Joe tell Mary I am here if she needs anything, I mean anything I'm so sorry, so very sorry."

She left and stumbled her way home thinking of the fair-haired young lad with the freckles on his nose and the impish grin, which she would never see again. Oh how sad, she thought steadying herself against a lamppost trying to regain control. How very old and worn she felt. The war had already taken a huge toll and now another innocent life had been stolen.

****

The year was 1917 and the Germans stepped up all efforts in sinking the merchant ships bringing food supplies from Canada and the US. Their relentless onslaught across the Atlantic caused drastic shortages in Britain's food reserves bringing its subjects to near starvation. Food prices rose to an all-time high.

At the onset of war, Joe had started stock piling whatever he could in the cellar. He knew his neighbours ran the risk of starvation and determined to be in as good a position as possible to meet the needs of a desperate people. The more well-to-do were well supplied because they could afford to pay the black market prices but the poor did not have enough food to sustain themselves. Gardens and any spare land were taken over to growing anything edible, even a few chickens were being raised. One year before the war ended, the government commissioned over two million acres for the growing of produce and because all the young men who normally worked the land had been conscripted, the Women's Land Army was formed. These women made an enormous contribution to the war effort, manning farm equipment and working the land producing vegetables and fruit. Even though their contribution was significant, there was still a chronic food shortage with wheat at an all-time low because of the constant bombing and loss of the supply ships. Rationing of food was then implemented.

Lyza found the concept of the Women's Land Army wholly encompassing. Over 100,000 women enrolled. The farm work was heavy and the women were not readily welcomed as some farmers thought they were not physically strong enough to handle the load; nevertheless, they were proven wrong. The women's work was a major and invaluable contribution, their impact and participation in the war effort immeasurable. Lyza was so proud albeit sad that she had been unable to make such a contribution.

The months passed and previous enthusiasm died in the hearts of those left on the home front. So many dead and the injured brought into the London train stations at night so as not to raise too much concern, to be disbursed to various parts of England. The devastating toll the war was taking could not be hidden and morale reached an all-time low. Inflation climbed ever higher and the poor got poorer. Lyza struggled. She was grateful for the few clients she had with her music lessons and then there was her dressmaking and laundry services to make ends meet.

The work situation for women was slightly eased by the war effort. Because of the huge shortage of men more and more women were entering the work force into unionized work. The only previous employment for lower class women had been working as domestics in service for middle class families. Lyza had been spared that, although she still provided some domestic services. The migration of women to 'trades' positions resulted in a shortage of women in service; consequently they were in high demand. Lyza had been offered several positions but they were live-in and even when she had been offered work enabling her to leave at the end of the day to go to her own home, the hours were long and it was unthinkable anyway with a child to care for. So she struggled on.

She noted wryly that women once again were 'getting the rough end of the stick'. Even though there was more work available for them and training in more technical jobs, they were hired only on a temporary basis and expected to resume their roles as housewives and mothers or work as domestics after the end of the war. There was still animosity directed towards female workers as it was not deemed correct for a woman to replace a man in any male dominated job; therefore, employers took full advantage of the situation and hired several women to do the job of one man. They worked small segments of his job and were therefore paid at a lower rate. The hours were long and the pay far from equal.

Women fought a long fight for equality but it was not until the mid-1920s that they won the right to vote and new equal opportunity regulations were put in place.

There were some good times though throughout these troubled years. One day Lyza was sitting in the park waiting to meet Olive from one of her music classes, when an older gentleman sat down wearily beside her. He smiled weakly and they exchanged some pleasantries, although it was hard to find pleasant words in such miserable times. His name was Edward Brown and they introduced themselves formally.

"I have been looking for somewhere to live, somewhere reasonable. My wife passed on a while back and, and…" He stopped and turned away. Lyza noted his eyes were moist and waited while he groped for a handkerchief from his pocket and trying to appear nonchalant blew his nose soundly.

"It was my son you see, we lost him, got the word a few months ago. Killed the wife, she couldn't bear it, didn't want to live anymore." His anguish overtook him again.

"Come and have a cup of tea with me. I just have to pick up my niece we live just around the corner."

"Oh, I really can't impose," Edward said, having gained his composure.

"Yes you can and you must taste a piece of my gingerbread. I had just enough ingredients to make one and it's really good.

They walked together to the school and Olive was waiting outside the main entrance. Lyza gave her a quick hug and Edward noted how the girl displayed no emotion towards her aunt and wondered why. Undaunted, Lyza rambled on.

"Olive this is Mr. Edward Brown, he is coming home for tea and may possibly be renting out the room I was telling you about."

"That's nice," Olive said without conviction. "Do you mind if I go out later? I've done all my homework and want to meet some friends."

"We'll talk about that later, dear," her aunt replied decisively. "Come on, let's get along, it's getting late."

Edward had raised an eyebrow at the mention of the room to rent and interest peaked, he said, "What's this about a room, Lyza? Tell me about it."

"All in good time, Edward," she replied grinning broadly. "All in good time."

Chapter 7

Remembrance

She sat at the piano in the library and the beautiful strains filled the room. Running through her repertoire of music she settled on Mozart her favourite composer. Entering a world of serenity her thoughts centred on the music composed in the 1780s when Mozart was at his peak, so popular, revered in fact. Yes, she too would be revered. Her music would be known throughout England, no, possibly the whole world. Her thoughts ran amok for a while as she basked in the glory of true success and adulation.

She remembered the last concert where she had performed on the piano and smiled with pleasure, her face radiant. How different she appeared, beautiful in fact with her vivacious colouring, so alive, so dynamic. She saw them all again as if they were in the same room. How everyone clapped as they leapt to their feet and with unanimous roars of approval called her back on the stage over and over again.

Her fingers on the keys moved away from the world of serenity and entered the restless undertones of the music seemingly to match her changed mood. It was not that she really thought about it much, but the fact was she had been thrown away, cast out from the family. She had everything she could possibly want yet it never really seemed enough. She remembered again catching her brother's eye briefly at the concert. He immediately averted his gaze. Oh yes, Mr. Goody Frank, she thought viciously, I'll show you.

****

Frank was born the year after Olive and was doing very well at school, every effort being made to help him into a fine career. Already he showed leanings towards public service and it seemed he would be a strong contender. He never lost an opportunity to volunteer in local political campaigns and spared no effort helping out in the local campaign offices. Whenever and wherever possible, he gave little public speeches and everyone agreed he would be a strong contender in a few years. There were many issues on the political agenda at the time.

The war may have been over but a huge number of other serious problems emerged. Trades unions were becoming much more powerful with higher membership triggering more unrest. Many more work stoppages and strikes regarding prices, pay, alcohol control, too much overtime, excessive fatigue on the job, and inadequate housing were just a few of the crises that political powers had to resolve and young Frank certainly had a voice and was bent on being heard at every opportunity.

Once in a while Frank and Olive's paths crossed when they were performing at local events. Frank was an amazingly fine public speaker, given his young age and would recite short stories. His poetry lacked conviction and soul but his short stories held the audience, particularly when they involved some crime or had political implications. Whenever the two were forced to communicate, it was intolerably uncomfortable with a strong undertone of dislike which became progressively worse with each encounter. Her aunt always tried to smooth things out on these occasions, but Olive knew that, talented though she was it was never enough. She was snubbed again and again by her family.

Then there was that fatal concert when she had overheard her grandmother. Olive went cold when she thought of it. They were all there… Grandmother was saying "What an extremely talented girl. She must have inherited it from that gypsy father of hers. They're gifted musicians if nothing else, the thieving lot. How her mother could have got involved, God only knows… but I must say, she does have a beautiful voice and her piano playing is incredible." The old woman rambled on. "Of course, she obviously takes after him. Look at that raven black hair and the dark skin, not a bit like any of us."

Olive had recoiled in horror at the words which were to haunt her for ever more. Oh she would show them all right. Just wait. After the incident, she began to withdraw more and more, striving to do better and better in the arts areas. Yes, she would be the best at everything she did.

****

Olive allowed herself to become lost in her playing. The music left the restless and returned once again to the quiescent world, never failing to allow her to heal and renew herself. Finally, she shut the lid firmly over the keys and was readying up her music when her aunt knocked on the library door.

"Olive, don't forget your mother said she would drop by today. Perhaps you should get yourself ready; aren't you going to play your new piano recital for her? I know she will just love it."

I have no wish to do anything for her, least of all something to make her happy. She never thought about me did she?" Olive replied sullenly.

"Come now, Olive, that's not true, let's not get into that again. She was too poor; they just couldn't manage to keep you. That's not to say they didn't love you and still do."

"Oh, don't gloss it over. I'm well aware of the situation. I know I don't have the same dad as Frank. I overheard grandmother and the rest of them talking about me at the last concert." She brushed past Lyza and went on upstairs with a flourish to her room.

Lyza heard the door slam and sighing moved over to the patio door and surveyed the garden striving to calm herself. Well that was unfortunate, hearing her grandmother mouthing off like that; poor girl she must have been so shocked. Well too late now, the damage is done, best just to leave it alone now. She was at her wits end, already her funds were depleting with the costs of rearing Olive. Food rationing of items such as meat, sugar and fats had been instigated in 1918 following the war. Fortunately bread was still available. Whenever meat was to hand, it was customary to save the drippings after cooking and live off this for days, using it almost like butter by spreading it on bread. Lyza's mouth watered at the thought of the dripping sandwiches, mmm lovely with lots of pepper. Then there was the bread pudding with cinnamon and dried fruit if available. Her spirits lifted.

Back in her room, Olive made herself look presentable and gathered up what she thought was appropriate music for the occasion of her mother's visit. Thank goodness I'll be free of this soon, she thought. I'm out of here at the first opportunity. She heard the door go downstairs and then her aunt was calling up to her that her mother had arrived. I'd better get down there she thought. Maybe it'll be a short gathering; I'll move things along as quickly as I can. She was anxious not to delay the visit. Hopefully she'd be able to slip away later and conclude the little business transaction she had been working on. Pausing for a moment her thoughts ran through recent events.

****

She had taken to hanging around the local pubs for some time and discovered her music and singing was well received. Although under age, she appeared and acted well beyond her 15 years. Sam the proprietor of one of the pubs obviously had a 'thing' for her and she thought she would turn it to her advantage. She had played the piano once in a while just for a laugh but she had been so well received that it occurred to her she could possibly earn a few shillings here and there. She was truly delighted when Sam had suggested just that. She had been sitting enjoying a shandy one evening when Sam sidled up and fondled the back of her neck.

"You know, darlin', you really make the old ivories sing and you're not half bad to look at neither. 'Ow would you like to play a few rounds once in a while? It would bring in the customers and make you a bit of cash. They just love a bit of a sing song and I'm sure they'll be generous with the tips."

Olive had lowered her eyes and then looked up bewitchingly, leading him on, making the most of the moment.

"Well, Sam, it's like this, I don't come cheap. I've had a lot of professional training and while I would love to play for the boys, there has to be something worthwhile in it for me you know."

"Of course, of course, I get your drift." Sam spoke hastily not wishing to lose his advantage. "Why don't we sit down and work out the details, let's set a date, just you and me and we'll get down to the nitty-gritty of the thing."

"OK, Sam, what about next Monday?" she said, flirting with him outrageously. She knew Lyza went to see Gertrude on Mondays and always being tired from a full day, usually slept when she got home. Sam nodded in agreement and, kissing him lightly on the cheek just to get him going and hurrying to her feet, she headed towards the door.

"I really have to go now, thanks for the drink. I'll see you Monday. Make sure you've got the pounds shillings and pence clear in your mind for when I come and we should talk about the scheduling, as well." Then with a toss of her beautiful black hair, she was gone.

That night, walking home she was elated thinking of the events of the evening. I'll take it slowly, get my feet wet so to speak and then I'll see if I can squeeze free board out of that randy so and so, she thought coldly.

Olive slipped away from school more and more frequently. She began to take inventory of what she was going to need in the way of clothes and other personal items and just simply took what she wanted.

One day while wandering around one of the shops, she had narrow escape as she headed towards the door. The store detective had become curious because she was in the store frequently and never seemed to buy anything. On this particular day, she headed briskly for the door with another blouse tucked out of sight. When confronted, she gave her usual elaborate spiel, laced with charm. The security guard was completely taken in by her beguiling manner and feeling rather embarrassed at having thought the girl had been shoplifting, he stepped aside allowing her to pass.

"I could have sworn I saw her lift a blouse," he said under his breath. "I'll just be on the lookout for her in the future. Obviously I'll have to catch her red-handed to put a stop to it."

They can afford it, Olive thought, as she hurried away, absolving herself of any guilt, it's all a matter of survival of the strongest. After the incident, she moved her operations around so as not to draw suspicion upon herself. She acquired an impressive wardrobe.

****

Pulling herself up with a jolt, she put the finishing touches to her hair. Not bad she thought, peering in the mirror, no outstanding! Smiling, she picked up her music and went downstairs to prepare for her mother's visit.

****

Martha hurried down the road; she was going to visit Olive and Lyza. She stopped dead in her tracks. Once again steeped in past memories, she found herself imprisoned in those deep eyes, which she had never forgotten. He, too, held her to him and momentarily they became as one locked in their own moment in time. He said her name softly and tearing her gaze away, the pain in her chest unimaginable, she turned and stumbled up the garden path of Lyza's home. She dare not look back but his presence enfolded her.

Lyza showed Martha to the parlour where she sank into the old wing chair. Her heart was pounding and closing her eyes she could see his face again, feel the softness of his kiss and sense again his urgency. She felt the strength of their love once more flowing through her veins. She had allowed herself this indulgence only on the rarest of occasions. The pain of remembrance was too overwhelming, too much to bear. She felt as if she were about to faint and without warning, the tears flowed and she gave herself up to them, sobbing as if even her very soul was breaking apart. Hearing Lyza coming down the hall with the tea trolley, she made a huge effort to regain control and was dabbing her eyes when the door opened. Lyza being the angel she was said nothing, almost as if she understood what had transpired. Excusing herself on the pretext of preparing something in the kitchen she left her sister to recover herself fully but couldn't help noticing how thin and worn Martha was, she simply didn't eat enough and it was beginning to tell on her.

Martha was grateful for the tea and fresh home baked goodies which her sister was always able to produce on any occasion it seemed. Sipping her tea she revelled in the peace and warmth the room exuded, bathing in the incandescent glow the old lamp cast. Her body ached with fatigue. Her visits to see Olive had become increasingly stressful; her daughter obviously felt no love only deep-seated resentment towards her. Martha had long since lost the zest for living and made her way through the days like a zombie, just pleasing the family, ignoring her own needs; there was never time for her anyway and nobody seemed to notice. Her daughter's feelings towards her were just more heartbreak to overcome.

Following Olive's birth, there had been little respite from child-bearing for Martha. Bert was merciless and his drinking out of control. There was no avenue of escape. Martha took comfort in the fact that her second-born, Frank, was doing well at school now and she really enjoyed going to the local gatherings and hearing him speak. He spent every waking moment helping out with various political campaigns, delivering pamphlets, etc.

She recalled the last gathering of local talent she was able to attend. It was a rare occasion for her as she was overwhelmed with household chores and trying to earn a few pounds. She walked slowly towards the church hall, always a little apprehensive at these gatherings, wishing to avoid too much involvement with the locals. Choosing a seat at the back near the door she glanced around. Her mother in law was seated a few rows down. She noted Lyza had just arrived with Olive and Gertrude. Lyza was speaking to Olive who seemed totally unaware or disinterested; her eyes roamed restlessly around the audience falling on her mother's face. Martha's smile of encouragement fell on barren ground. She shuddered as she did every time she saw the closed vacant expression directed at her. Olive straightened herself up as if to pull herself back to the present and with a flicker of a smile, turned her back and hurried to the stairs leading behind the stage to get ready for her performance.

The audience was in awe, clapping wildly after Olive's performance. The girl's face lit up as she accepted her praise and paraded around the stage responding to numerous encores. Following her recital she made her way off the stage. She didn't attempt to join her mother or Lyza but stood quietly in the wings to the side of the audience. Frank was next to give a rendition on public support to the local MP. A little dry but Frank made his point and always held the audience's attention. During his performance, Martha's gaze fell upon her daughter again. The girl was standing a short distance behind her grandmother. Her grandmother was deeply engrossed in conversation with some members of her family and obviously unaware of her granddaughter's presence. Olive's face was ashen. Martha concluded that it must be the animosity she felt towards her brother, strange though that the girl's expression of hatred seemed to be directed towards her grandmother.

Following the performances Martha made a quick exit before the crowds left their seats. If I hurry, she thought, there'll be time for a walk by the river.

****

Martha startled, jumped forward in her seat to greet Olive who came across with her music sheets. My goodness, how she's grown, thought Martha, almost a woman. The girl didn't bother with any pleasantries, just a curt greeting.

"What would you like to hear Mother? What would you like me to play?"

That settled, Martha sat back and tried to relax. She closed her eyes and allowed the piano's clear tones to wash over her.

Again she heard the river bubbling and eddying over the rocks and she was home, encircled in his arms, home with the meadows redolent of sweet grasses and flowers. Home with the senses intoxicated by the smells and sounds pervading the air. Shadows began to lengthen and an iridescent but chilly mist crept over the waves. Martha shuddered and clasping her outmoded coat around her slender body, pulled away and leapt to her feet. "I have to go," she whispered desperately.

****

The music had stopped and Martha became aware of Olive's penetrating scrutiny. "That was so beautiful Olive," she said, wrenching herself back into the present. "You play so exquisitely."

Chapter 8

Olive departs

Olive sat toying with her drink. The night was slow getting underway and she thought she would wait until a larger crowd appeared before seating herself at the piano. Business had been very good for her, what with the free drinks she cajoled her way into and the tips dropped in her dish on the piano, not to mention those of the more amorous who would stop behind her taking every opportunity she afforded them to look down her dress and finally stuff a few notes down her cleavage. "Yes, life is good," she murmured to herself. "I must see Sam about finalizing a room then I can really clean-up, what with the lunch crowd as well." As if he had read her mind, Sam suddenly appeared, ogling at her as he made his way across the bar.

"Hello, darlin'," he said huskily as he grabbed her. Olive disengaged herself.

"Now, Sam, what about the room; is anything available yet?"

"You're in luck, babe, a tenant is moving out at the end of the month. It's a good room and it has your name on the door."

Olive was euphoric and reciprocated with a huge hug of which Sam took full advantage, as usual. Aware that the pub had started to fill up and patrons were jostling for seats at the bar, Olive became restless and shaking Sam off one arm and a slightly inebriated individual off the other, she hastened to her feet.

"Right then, Sam, time I started making a bit of the old ready, there's a crowd gathering and I don't want to miss out. As a special favour, sweetheart, I'll play the next piece for you."

Sam leered and following one last fondle swaggered closer to the piano for a better view, scowling over his shoulder at the amorous individual who was trying to pick himself up from the floor having fallen off his stool when Olive had disengaged him as she left the bar area.

Olive was in her element and ran her fingers up and down the keys as was her customary warm-up, far removed from her professional training. Sometimes she thought wryly if it's 'honky-tonk' they want, let them have it. Half-way through her rendition, she cast her eye around and for just a few seconds locked eyes with the stranger, yet again. He sat quietly nursing his beer at the bar, deep in thought. “What’re we drinking, gypsy?” she addressed him insolently. He looked at her knowingly and left abruptly leaving his beer hardly touched. She felt mildly uncomfortable upon meeting his gaze for a second as he closed the door behind him. The incident was soon forgotten, however, as she pounded out the songs her audience wanted to hear and plied her trade wherever she thought she could make a few pounds.

****

“You can’t keep me here any longer,” screamed Olive. “I’ll be sixteen shortly and I’m out of here. I’ve rented accommodation and am guaranteed work. So that’s that and there’s nothing more to say.”

Lyza fought to remain on her feet. The shock of such venomous animosity directed at her, thrown in her face so cruelly, was more than she could bear. Edward came to her aid and if it had not been for his strong arm, her legs would have failed her. Olive swept out of the room with one last blazing look leaving Edward and Lyza alone.

Gently but firmly Edward led Lyza to the library. “Come now, dear, let’s sit you by the window. Calm yourself, my sweet, everything will be just fine.”

Lyza felt the comfort of the deep winged chair and allowed her body to sink into it, luxuriating in the deep brocade pile of Jacobean style. The chair had been around as long as she could remember and had always instilled a sense of security and well-being.

Edward re-appeared with a small glass brandy in each hand. “Here, girl, get this down you, this will make you feel more like it,” he said, leaning over to hand her the drink. When he too was comfortably settled he raised his glass. “Here’s to you, dear Lyza, you have given so unselfishly to just about every human being that has come your way. Don’t reproach yourself my dear, life is volatile and some things can’t be changed by anybody. Olive must do her own thing and follow her self-destructive course. You laid the groundwork, gave her every opportunity, the rest is up to her.”

Lyza raised her glass. “And to you, dear Edward, who have been so supportive and enabled me to carry on through these grim times, you will always have a place in my heart.”

They sat for a while enjoying their quietude. These times were their anchor, their base where each drew strength from the other.

Upstairs Olive began flinging her clothes into piles and reached for two holdalls. I’ll make a start on this, she thought, there will be less to do at the end of the month. Perhaps I'll check with Sam and see if he could store some of my belongings in the interim.

The next couple of weeks seemed to drag for Olive. She moved some of her possessions and by this time was spending most of her time at the pub. There was no further discussion on the subject; Lyza being totally out of her depth was resigned to her ward's imminent departure and the girl's fiercely defensive attitude, determined to do things her way.

One evening Olive burst upon Lyza and Edward in the library, immediately shattering their tranquillity. "Well, I'm off," she spoke crisply and with a slight softening of her voice, "Auntie, don't worry about me, I am just fine and this is what I want. I'll drop by and see you and let you know how I am getting along." With that, she was gone. Her choice to leave a life full of promise and opportunity which her brilliance and talent would have afforded her. The seamy side of life and all its lurid offerings was to be her stage and she was all too eager to get her show on the road.

****

Olive settled into her new life very easily and amazingly felt quite at home in the seedy rooms above the bar, with the equally seedy tenants of questionable nature. Even the shared bathroom with its unsanitary cracked appliances, situated at the end of the dark hallway with its torn and faded carpet which had seen better days, didn't seem to bother her.

Yes, she slotted into her new routine quickly and efficiently, accruing quite a sum of working cash which she had acquired from various people's pockets. She would pause her piano playing and mingle amongst the drinkers, throwing them off guard with her beautiful voice, becoming adept at relieving them of small sums. It amused her to imprison them in her sultry gaze and when she had them completely captivated, would stealthily palm wallets and/or cash swiftly and move on to the next victim. Should she happen to get lucky with a wallet, she would excuse herself to go to the washroom to hide her spoils. A favourite spot was always behind the plumbing, surface mounted on the walls in the older run-down public houses. She would go back later when the coast was clear and 'ferret' the goods away.

Olive always made her biggest hauls when Mona and the 'girls' were around. They were a gang of local prostitutes that hung out together, occasionally swapping so-called clients and relieving them of everything they could get their hands on. Generally, they worked the seedy, run-down public houses singly but occasionally traded their wares as a group at parties, business gatherings, etc. Olive was always glad to see Mona, knowing that she could make a killing, as she was on safe ground, the other's reputation preceding her, thus diverting suspicion from herself. There was always a bit of a scramble when the police raided the place following complaints from outraged customers who found their pockets empty and their wallets, watches and anything marketable, missing. The women were then lined up and searched for stolen goods. Olive usually had someone who was 'in her pocket' posted strategically who would give her the heads up shortly before the invasion and apologizing profusely, with a variety of excuses she would exit quickly through the back door seconds before the raid.

She became well-known at all the local pawn shops, the proprietors always glad to see her with her wealth of goodies namely jewellery and watches. Their 'claw-back' didn't seem to bother her either, as long as she made a few pounds, she didn't care whether she was being short-changed or not. Occasionally though, she would haggle, if she had originally brought in a piece and later decided to buy it back usually because she had her own buyer. The proprietor was forced to make a concession, knowing it was better to cut her a little slack; they would always get it back and more next time she was in. Her home became all the seedy corners of the lower end of town; her associates the dregs of humanity and her trade, surpassed by none, that of a con and thief.

She saw the Romany every once in a while, but never addressed him again. She was always aware of his presence, however, and always felt a little uneasy. He would just watch her intently and occasionally when she sang a sentimental love song, his eyes would mist over and he would stumble out of the pub. Sometimes, just because she was inclined, she would deliberately sing some heart-breaking ballad of lost love just to see the man's reaction and give herself a little boost, fully cognizant of her power and ability to reduce him to such depths of sadness.

There was one night, however, when slipping into her other psyche of quality and serenity she began playing 'In a Monastery Garden', a light classical piece composed by Albert W. Ketelbey in the early 1900s. The gypsy drew close to the piano and together they vocalized raising their voices to the heavens as if both were in some ancient medieval church singing to their God. Their audience, filled with awe, fell silent, every person wholly absorbed. Tears fell freely from the eyes of both gypsy and the young woman at the piano; their choir-like tones so pure, harmonizing so perfectly in concert with each other. Many in the lounge bar, overwhelmed by the moment, shamelessly shed their own tears, so utterly lost were they in the haunting strains. It was as if Olive was hypnotized and everyone else along with her but just as suddenly she changed the tempo and 'honky tonk' once again rang through the rafters. Drinks started flowing and the drinkers, slightly abashed, resumed their usual crudities. Their eyes met; it was their epiphany and in that moment of truth both gypsy and young woman were fully cognisant of what each was to the other. Roman slipped quietly away.

Chapter 9

WW1 ends

Lyza was once again in her favourite spot in the garden. She sat there whenever there was a spare moment which was not often. The garden was once again working its magic reviving her spirit, bestowing calmness upon her. Those were such good years, she thought. Edward had made it possible for her to continue. She shifted her position on the wooden bench. It was proving a bit hard on her bony frame, as she had forgotten to bring out her cushion but she wasn't going to go indoors for it, she just wanted to sit.

Dear Edward, what a good man you've been all these years, she thought with fondness. Never have you taken advantage, always so quiet, so unassuming. What a wonderful companion you've been to me.

Once again, she was drawn to that first day when Edward had come into her life and he had sat in her kitchen looking so forlorn.

****

The old house looked welcoming, beckoning to them it seemed, as they rounded the corner. Lyza turned the big brass key in the lock and showed them into the spacious hallway. "Olive, pop upstairs and get yourself organized. I'm putting a pot of tea on the hob. I'll call you when it's ready." Olive made no reply and headed upstairs. Edward noted the girl's ill humour and lack of respect for her aunt but said nothing. Lyza's face was quite serene and he concluded that she had grown accustomed to being treated in such a way and had learned to brush it off.

After hanging up their coats, Lyza showed Edward into the parlour.

"There, sit yourself down and I'll bring in the tea," and as an afterthought she said, "Wait, would you like anything to read? Why don't I show you the library and you can make a selection to browse through while you're waiting for refreshments?"

Edward followed her to the back of the house and into the library. "Oh how magnificent," he gasped, "Oh what a beautiful room and my goodness look at all the literature."

Lyza, smiling appreciatively, beckoned.

"Yes, it's my favourite room in the house. Come with me let's take a quick look at the garden before I go and put the tea on."

Standing outside the French doors, Lyza noted Edward's face took on a distant look; removed to another world, he was lost in the moment, devouring every aspect of the garden, just as she did every time she laid her eyes on it. She left quietly, allowing him his own space.

Later they sat silently sipping their tea. The gingerbread had gone down very well and Lyza was gratified that Edward wasted not a crumb. Olive had taken her tea upstairs saying she wanted to look over some music.

"I can't help but notice that Olive doesn't seem a particularly happy child," Edward remarked breaking the silence suddenly. Lyza looked at him keenly.

"Oh, Edward, it's a long story but she has good reason to be the way she is. Although sometimes I feel I've taken on too much. I'm her guardian you see and it falls to me to rear her as well as I can."

"Well, she seems to be doing very well and obviously wants for nothing."

"Now, Edward, tell me more about what you were hoping to find with regard to new lodgings and where are you living now?" said Lyza changing the subject, not wanting the ambiance of the moment violated.

"My accommodation is on a week-to-week basis. I'm renting a room close to Olive's school. It has a small scullery which I share with a couple of other tenants but it's hard making food, nowhere proper to store it and things go missing, you see. I was well placed but what with the war and losing our boy and then Kerry just giving up and dying."

Edward's voice cracked as he re-lived the horror of it all.

"I have a good job with the London and South Western Railway. It's just that I've lost myself, you see, I can't get motivated anymore. I have a bit of savings in the bank and I'll get a bit of a pension shortly, so I should be able to get by if I can find reasonable accommodation and get out of that foul room with those obnoxious people."

Lyza busied herself clearing the plates. "Why don't I show you the room I am thinking of renting out. My previous tenant left a short while ago and my cousin is always telling me to sub-let if things get too tough and believe me, things are getting too tough. I would be offering a room and board at a reasonable rent with some light handyman duties. That's why I was going to advertise for a quiet businessman on his own who would like to keep his hand in and keep himself fit with a little work such as help in the garden and minor repairs and maintenance. Come, I'll show you round the rest of the house and you must stay for supper, just to get a feel for things. Of course, I would have to contact Herbert if you're interested, he's my cousin's lawyer; he handles everything connected with Olive and my living accommodation."

They looked over the house and returned to the library; Lyza settled him in the large wing chair. "There now while I go and make dinner, you sit and think a while and go over the details in your mind. After dinner, we'll take a quick walk through the garden and you can let me know how you feel."

Edward took her hand and, voice shaking, stumbling over his words he said quietly, "Lyza, you are so wonderful, so kind, it would be an honour and privilege for me to live in this wonderful home."

"Well then, that's settled, I'll get in touch with Herbert in the morning. He'll set out the rental agreement," she said with conviction.

****

The robin trilling loudly wrenched her back for a few moments to watch him cavorting along the wall trying to get her attention it seemed and it worked, his antics captured her full attention and a warm smile lit up her face. “Little Robin, you’re such a clown.” She chastised him gently. Once again the discomfort of the bench was getting the better of her and taking off her woollen shawl she stood and arranged it as a cushion. Settling back down, once again her mind straddled the years.

****

The four-year course of the war had taken its toll with Britain and France suffering even more casualties than Germany. Thank God for the British Red Cross, she thought. Their amalgamation with the Order of St. John formed the Joint War Committee operating under the umbrella of the Red Cross at the onset of the war. The value of their work was incalculable. They were not only fully trained in caring for the sick and wounded but also circulated amongst the sick and dying boosting morale.

Finally, on 11 November 1918, the war was over. The singing and dancing in the streets was infectious. Lyza was to remember it all the days of her life. The losses were in excess of 990,000 of military and civilian and over 7 million had passed through Hampshire on their way to the front.

The following Sunday in church the congregation hung their heads in humility and thanked God for bringing the fighting to an end. There were many tears shed that day and memorial services for the loss of hundreds of young Hampshire souls whose families would never forget and in many cases never forgive.

Lyza and Edward sat together. Joe and Mary were in the second row, heads bowed in grief, thinking of their lad with the lopsided grin always acting the clown who would never bring laughter to their home again. Grief and anguish permeated the air. Edward too bowed his head and his thoughts were with the loss of his young son and his dear wife. We may have gained the victory but at what a huge cost; what a terrible loss, he thought sadly. He reached for Lyza's hand and they sat quietly overwhelmed with sadness. All those young lives gone, snuffed out, what a terrible waste. How would England ever recover from this horror? Tears washed the faces of all present as unabashed they surrendered to their feelings. The entire congregation, without exception joined unanimously in their suffering.

That night Lyza and Edward sat on the bench in the lee of the wall. The night air was fresh on their cheeks and Edward held her in his arms and comforted her tenderly.

"Lyza my dear, we'll get through this together."

What an unselfish man, she thought for the umpteenth time, with all that he has suffered, losing his son, then his wife and he still is able to think of the likes of me. They had finally walked arm in arm towards the house, finding peace and solace in each other.

Another battle began in England to restore some kind of regular routine in the day to day living. The war had triggered widespread industrial unrest; some industries being much harder hit than others. The re-building and development of Southampton docks and one of the greatest stations in the world, Waterloo Station, which had handled the humungous amount of traffic of World War 1, created more work through the railway, particularly as suburban lines were now electrified with power signalling. Many workers; however, were displaced, which resulted in a stronger recognition of union management and more union membership in efforts to secure jobs. Work stoppages and strikes were rampant and the fight for lower prices, abolishment of alcohol control, higher pay and less hours pitted worker against worker.

There were ongoing problems for women in the work force. Those that were married were boycotted. So many women were widowed or single with no source of income. The fight for the jobs was underway and finally resolutions were passed prohibiting married women from entering certain working environments. Lyza followed the women's rights movements avidly, knowing that it was too late for her to actively participate but the politics were a constant stimulating source of interest to her.

Joe had suffered huge declines in his business. Food supplies were short because of the loss of so many supply ships. People were going out into the country to pick up produce from the farms, by the time it hit the shops it was top price. The British public were able to afford less and less. Because of the hardship and against Joe's will, Mary was forced to seek employment.

One night she was walking home when a group of women cornered her in an alley. "There she is the greedy cow, taking work away from those that need it. She's got a man, what about the rest of us that's lost ours. Let's teach her a lesson," one of them screamed hysterically. "Let's get her." Poor Mary didn't have a chance. There were four of them, reduced to the lowest ranks of humanity; they beat her into the ground her screams falling on barren ground. When she finally lay motionless, as with all bullies, they took their leave lest they should be seen and identified for the evil creatures that they were. Mary slipped in and out of consciousness bathed in her own blood.

Back at the shop Joe was getting more and more distressed, wondering where his wife was. Finally he grabbed his coat and set off to look for her. I should have been more insistent when I told her I would meet her from work. Oh Mary, Mary why are you so stubborn he thought. He quickened his pace and rounded the corner to cut through the alley. His eyes fell on what looked like a dishevelled heap of clothing and as he drew nearer the horror became reality when he realized it was his wife, covered in blood, motionless in the gutter. He rushed to her aid, and taking her into his arms, rocked her gently feeling as if his heart was being ripped from his body. Burying his head in her soft hair, crying like a baby absolutely sure that his wife was dead, he cried over and over again.

"Oh Mary, my sweet Mary, dear God, please don't take her, please give us a little more time."

Suddenly he felt a slight movement and opening his eyes awash with tears, he looked into her sweet face. Her blue eyes returned his stare and a flicker of a smile passed over her lips. "Oh thank God," he almost shrieked and with a surge of brute strength, lifted her up in his arms. "Mary darling, let's get you home."

Joe went to Lyza for help; she was just clearing up after dinner when the doorbell sounded. Lyza opened the door and there was Joe standing on the threshold in an appalling state. "Lyza, please can you help?" He was gasping for breath in his anguish. "It's Mary." Once again he buried his face in his hands.

"Joe, tell me, please tell me." Lyza yelled as she grabbed for her coat. "Edward," she shouted, "Edward are you there?" Edward appeared almost immediately and Joe, getting himself together, relayed the incident. They were both aghast.

"Lyza, go immediately with Joe, don't worry about Olive or anything here, I'll take charge and 'man the ship' until you get back."

Lyza grabbed Joe's arm and together they rushed up the street.

In the weeks that followed, Lyza went every day to wash and tend to Mary's needs. She did some light housekeeping and prepared a meal for the family before she left each day. Poor Mary, such a good person; why was it that the best of people seemed to come in for the worst? The routine was gruelling for Lyza who was always up at dawn. She had her dressmaking clients to tend to, making deliveries and picking up new jobs, along with preparing meals for Edward and Olive and maintaining the house. She also tutored several music students during the course of each month and had her regular pupils and regular drop-ins referred to her by word of mouth. The added burden of taking care of Mary was beginning to show and Lyza was suffering from extreme exhaustion, it was only her indomitable spirit that kept her going.

****

Lyza shuddered, partly in remembrance and also a chill was settling over the garden. Thank goodness Mary was feeling moderately better. She was much stronger now and able to do more for herself. Lyza gathered up her embroidery and hurried to the house. Joe and Mary were coming to dinner and she had much to do.

Later she prepared her famous berry pie. Each year she would go to the Common to gather berries for her preserves. If it was a good season, she would manage to stretch the fruits throughout the winter months. Good preparation was essential to the success of her dinners. Money was always short and storing her concoctions ensured a good variety throughout the year. Mary and Joe were long-standing friends; she'd known them since school days. They had married when they were very young and their love for each other ever enduring.

Edward appeared at the door of the kitchen. "Is there anything I can do to help?" he enquired. Lyza handed him a soft cloth.

"Would you be a dear and polish the glasses? I have already set them out in the parlour. Make sure they are crystal clear; we'll sit by the fire after dinner and enjoy a little mulled wine it's so warming."

Lyza was proud of her homemade berry wine which she served warm with a variety of spices. Edward moved off swiftly to the parlour where the group would gather, he thought he would check out the fire and anything else in the room to heighten the welcome of their guests.

"Lyza, you've surpassed yourself once again, a meal fit for the gentry," said Joe.

"Yes, you're truly amazing," echoed Mary. "Come let me help you clear the kitchen." She shooed the men in the direction of the parlour. "You two go along, Lyza and I will join you shortly." With that she reached for the little two-shelved dinner trolley and began to stack the crockery ready for washing in the kitchen.

"Lyza sit down and rest a while," said Mary as she put the last of the dishes to drain. Obliging Lyza sat gratefully.

"Oh Mary I don't know what will become of Olive," she said. "The situation just goes from bad to worse. She's involved with those awful people; how could she be so wayward? I worry about her all the time and it's just as if I don't exist anymore, she seems to have forgotten me completely."

Lyza's voice broke and her eyes grew moist as they always did when she thought of what had become of the child she had cared for and nurtured all through the years.

Mary rushed to her friend's side and hugged her, "Lyza please don't," she soothed. "Just don't think about it. Things could turn around. She's still very young."

Lyza brightened at the encouragement and jumped to her feet.

"You're right, let's go and join the men and have a nice warming drink; we'll all enjoy that."

Later, having exhausted all conversation and being well fed, warm and content, they all sat quietly contemplating life around the fire. What a memorable evening.

Chapter 10

Too many kids

The year was 1923. Olive had been living away from Lyza for three years. She was, as usual, sitting at the bar in the pub taking a rest from the piano, feeling more than a little jaded, her late nights and racketing around were beginning to tell on her. She was thinking about Jake and their first meeting. Now there was a man what a pity things hadn't worked out.

****

That night, as now, Olive was taking a break when suddenly she was aware of a man taking the stool beside her. Filled with curiosity she glanced to her side and was immediately rewarded with a very knowing wink. That was the beginning of a relationship she thought would go on forever. Jake was such a good looking man, a pleasure to be seen around and Olive was completely obsessed with him.

One night in her room after Jake had gone down the hall to the bathroom, her eye fell on his wallet. As usual she couldn't resist and upon opening the wallet, to her horror saw a picture of him and a short, fair-haired smiling woman. She turned the photograph over and noted his writing on the back, 'My darling wife with me at Bournemouth, a weekend to remember.' Stricken with rage she thought, I'll show him, the two timing swine.

When he returned she said, "Jake honey, I accidently knocked your wallet on the floor and this fell out. Why didn't you mention you had a wife, for all I know there could be kids involved as well?"

"Oh God," he swore under his breath. "I meant to tell you but I never got around to it, the timing was never right. We haven't been getting along but times are so bad I couldn't leave her, you see and no, there are no kids involved."

"Well you're going to have to choose between us. That's all I can say. You'd better get rid of her or there's no more us."

Jake tried to talk to her several times after that but the reply was always the same: "Get rid of her, Jake," was all she would say.

Even though it was early afternoon, the previous night had been busy for Olive. She was not an early riser at the best of times and was still in her dressing gown. She went downstairs to pick up the local paper. Mesmerized she found herself staring into the face of the young woman she had seen in the photograph in Jake's wallet. The girl's body had been washed up on the beach. Foul play had not been determined.

"Oh Lord, it looks like he went and did her in," she said under her breath. "Could that be, did he really get rid of her just for me?" She felt a little flutter of gratification. "Oh what a compliment; he must have really taken a shine to me."

The police enquiry continued over the next few weeks and although more than a little tense when questioned, Olive put on her usual good show.

"Oh no officer I hardly knew him. We had a drink once in a while but that was all."

The death was deemed accidental, although always shrouded with suspicion.

Jake disappeared shortly after the investigation and Olive never heard from him again. She breathed a sigh of relief.

****

Yes it's a pity things hadn't worked out she thought as she returned to the piano. A group of railway workers came in and made their way to the bar and Olive immediately perked up. Hitting the keys, she burst into song, focussing her attention on one man in particular. He was very well built with huge shoulders and firm set chin. Oh I could certainly go a few rounds with him, she thought. Sure enough her flirtation bore fruit and given the green light, he immediately made his way to the piano.

"What are you drinking, darling?" he enquired enthusiastically.

"Oh how kind," she cooed. "I'll have a gin and tonic, a double," she hastily added. "Now, sweetheart, what would you like to hear?"

He was enraptured; she totally won him over. They arranged to get together the next time he was on leave.

Their outings would always follow the same pattern, grab a bite to eat and 'pub crawl' throughout the town or if she was working, Victor would position himself close to the piano completely besotted. Following a whirlwind courtship they were married in 1924.

Francis was born within the first year and was the apple of her mother's eye. Olive came as near to happiness as she had ever been and for a while things seemed to stabilize a little for her. The novelty of the first child was wholly encompassing and Olive would sit in the rocking chair with her baby girl in her arms and sing lullabies. The child was beautiful with the same colouring as her mother, thick black curly hair. She was well looked after and Olive being very talented in needlecrafts made all her clothing and blankets, etc. As with her music, she never followed a formal sheet. She had developed the habit of playing by ear and her knitted creations evolved from a cursory glance at the illustrated pattern. She was such a strange personality, so domesticated on the one hand and so wayward on the other. She would sit perfectly content, her knitting needles clacking away with her budgerigar perched on one of the needles as she worked. How she loved that bird, laughing and chortling as his little wings flapped to keep his balance.

"Who's a pretty boy," she would say over and over again and he'd wag his little head from side to side. If a bird could smile, he certainly did.

She took great pride in getting the child and herself ready for strutting around the neighbourhood showing off to the neighbours. For the first time in her life she felt normal, as if she fitted in and had finally found her 'place'. She was well received at her Auntie Lyza's home. There was always a tasty tray of goodies from Lyza's pantry with all the trimmings for afternoon tea. Lyza would coo over the baby and admire her latest outfit.

“Olive you certainly are an accomplished knitter and sewer.” Lyza’s spirit rallied, this might be the making of the girl she thought privately.

Olive was filled with satisfaction, an emotion new to her. On these occasions; however, she still never missed a chance to help herself to any items such as jewellery or little Victorian ornaments, usually beautiful little birds with brightly coloured eyes. Olive had always fostered a special liking for birds, Finches and Canaries in particular fascinated her and their beautiful singing always brought a smile. She had absolutely no compunction about taking anything that appealed to her and the little bird ornaments held particular intrigue for her. Always justifying her actions, she would think to herself, well the old lady has no need of these things, they’ll look much better in my room.”

The second year Olive’s second daughter was born, named Wanda followed by a boy Dugan, then Maude, Belinda and Davina.

Francis was in her thirteenth year when she finally accepted the fact that she had a hearing disability which had been manifesting itself very gradually over the past few years. It had now become very obvious to her and she became adept at watching mouths and developed a combination of lip reading and guessing what was being said. Most of the time she was successful and if she really concentrated she could get by but because of her difficulties coupled with her low self-esteem, she became very much a loner. Nobody really noticed; they simply assumed she wasn't listening or indifferent; in any event everybody was far too busy surviving and from the time her brother was born the quality of life had deteriorated drastically.

Olive would take to her bed at regular intervals and wait for Francis to get home to tend to her needs. "Fran luv," she would whine, "I'm not feeling too good. Get us a cup of tea there's a good girl. As an afterthought, she would always add, "Fran darling, don't know what I'd do without you?"

One day Olive was definitely not feeling well. Weak and sick she dragged herself to bed. Francis came home to find her unconscious, lying in a blood-stained bed. She rushed to get the doctor.

The doctor was leaning over Olive in her hospital bed when she opened her eyes. "You're lucky to be alive, my girl", he said and grabbing her hand, "I'm sorry you lost the baby but you're going to be all right. There won't be any more kids for you though," he added seriously. "Now get some rest."

Olive turned her face into the pillow. She just wanted to withdraw from the world and as she fell asleep, her only thought was thank God, no more kids.

Chapter 11

WW2 begins

When Edward's company amalgamated with other railways in 1923 it became part of the Southern Railway with routes extending throughout the south of England. Edward didn't get lost completely in the shuffle but was transferred to a lower profile job in the operations office, not as grand as before but he still managed to get by reasonably and Lyza was certainly glad of the extra income she received from him for his lodging and keep.

"Lyza dear, you are going to have to slow down. I know you want to help anybody and everybody but you have to look to yourself now. If you don't care for yourself, how can you possibly look after anybody else?" Edward spoke softly.

They had gone up to the Common, a favourite outing for them and Edward learned to love it as much as Lyza. Encompassing over 300 acres of prime woodland, green spaces and abundant with wildlife, it never failed to enthral the two of them. Originally the acreage had been used to graze cows and poor families relied on it for berry picking and fire wood; horse-racing and hot air ballooning took place in later years. The Common became a public park officially in the mid-1800s. Also at that time 27 acres of it was turned over to what became known as the Old Cemetery situated in the southern-most part of the park.

Lyza had taken great delight in showing Edward the park on their excursions and he learned something new on every visit. She took him through the Old Cemetery and they wandered amongst the headstones most with beautiful sentiments and some with just a name and dates of their owner's lifespan. A long time previously Lyza had put her name down for a plot when she passed on. As with the garden, it was a place of absolute sublimity and serenity, renewing her physically and spiritually. Lyza wanted these grounds to be her final resting place and encouraged Edward to put his name down as well.

"Edward dear, the time we have together is brief; it would be wonderful to think that perhaps we could rest close to one another when we leave this earth."

Yes, I agree and it's such a beautiful place, I'll certainly look into it.

They paused to look at the headstones of the lost passengers of the great liner Titanic. These people were native to Southampton and although their bodies were never recovered, they were still remembered and their headstones placed in this most sacred place.

"I'm sure those people would be very happy that they are to be remembered in the hearts of their countrymen forever." Lyza spoke softly and Edward squeezing her hand nodded in agreement as he nudged her along the path.

"Lyza we'd best be getting back now, it's getting late. "What a perfect day it's been."

****

It was September 3, 1939 and Lyza and Edward sat motionless in the library, two very frail people, looking rather like a couple of Pickwick characters from Charles Dickens's novel, Mr. Pickwick. They were both wearing little black waistcoats with stiffly starched white collars on their shirts. Their tea, already prepared on the tray, remained untouched. Bodies held rigid with sombre expressions on their faces, they hung onto every word of Neville Chamberlain, the British Prime Minister.

The worst had come to fruition. The Prime Minister's words conveyed the dreaded message; Britain had declared war on Germany. The Minister spoke of Hitler's untruthful and dishonourable statements and his determined quest and ultimate invasion of Poland. He reaffirmed the strong allegiance of France and Britain in joining forces and going to Poland's defence. The Minister then called on all British subjects to comply with the government's plans and commit to carrying out their duties either as volunteers in the war effort or as active members of the Services. The Minister conveyed the strength of the British spirit and how they would not tolerate the atrocities being dictated and acted out by the Nazi regime. In conclusion, God's blessing was sought in the face of war and the fight for that which was right.

****

Lyza and Edward passed a very quiet day together in close companionship but each lost in their own thoughts. Their dinner was light for neither had much of an appetite. Lyza noted Edward's heavy tread on the stairs as he made his way to his bedroom in the early evening.

"Poor Man," she uttered under her breath. "He must be dwelling on his losses of the last war and so it goes on." She, too, overcome with weariness hurried to her bed, a welcome sight as she readied herself for sleep.

Christmas was a little different that year. Lyza was unable to put up her little tree with its lights. 'Black-out' regulations were in place. A dark sheet had to cover all windows after dark; a display of lights would make it too easy for the enemy to bomb the house.

"Well, she said to Edward as they sat down to a meagre meal on Christmas day, "We should think ourselves lucky; at least we have food on our plates. It might not be what we want but its sustaining and we do have a glass of sherry. Although," she added, "the Food Ministry are bringing in rationing of bacon and butter in January, so that's the start of it, not that we eat much bacon."

She rambled on trying to keep Edward's attention, but she was worried about him and had been for a while. He seemed to pick at his food these days, had not been himself for some time. He smiled at her across the table and she couldn't help but notice how pale his features were. After dinner she told him to go and sit by the fire and she would bring in some tea.

Olive dropped in for one of her rare visits on Boxing Day but she didn't stay long. She never did. Lyza noted wryly that nothing was missing that day. She was aware that every time Olive came to visit, little items disappeared, a little jewellery or perhaps an ornament. Maybe Olive was observing the sanctity of the season, or maybe nothing took her fancy. Lyza had given up wondering about the situation, as long as she had enough to sustain herself that was all she cared about. She made sure; however, never to leave her purse in sight. It was just too much of a temptation for the young woman; just asking for trouble.

Once Olive had left, Lyza and Edward, needing a breath of fresh air, walked arm in arm down to the little church to sing a few hymns and pass their salutations to their neighbours. The rest of the day and evening passed serenely.

****

Lyza brought the tea tray to the library. Edward looked so peaceful asleep in the big winged chair overlooking the garden. It seems a shame to disturb him; but his tea will get cold she thought as she placed the tray on the little table and gently touched Edward's arm. He didn't move and, stiffening, she gazed into his face. He was gone, she knew that, but her mind would not accept it. Sitting down in the neighbouring chair she studied his face, etching it into her brain so that she could hold onto him forever.

"Dear, dear Edward, my consort, my friend, what will I do without you?" She spoke sadly and wept for the loss of her companion and the precious moments they'd shared. Her little lace handkerchief was saturated in seconds, as silently with head bowed she cried. Even little Robin, singing his heart out at the window for his evening meal of cake crumbs, could not detract from her abject sadness.

Edward had left his instructions to be buried in the Old Cemetery where they had been so happy together.

Upon going through his things Lyza came across an envelope addressed to her and sitting down to steady herself, she read:

To my dearest Lyza, words cannot fully express what is in my heart and how much you mean to me. Your pure innocence and goodness have filled me with joy and love every moment we shared together. Take care, my sweet friend, and may God watch over you forever.

Shed no tear for me, now that I am gone.

Let sadness not weaken you, keep your spirit strong.

Let your mind wander down the trails we loved so much.

Let your thoughts linger in the beds of flowers we loved to touch.

Locked in your heart, forever, I will remain,

To be brought forth and remembered with happiness again.

So go you well and tread lightly, for I am there,

To eternity, good memories you and I will share. ©

Following Edward's death, the situation got worse financially. Lyza knew she would have to take in another lodger to make ends meet and finally let the room at far below the rental rate to a woman who had lost her entire family when their house had been bombed. She, too, would have lost her life, but she went to help a sick neighbour and was unfortunate enough to witness the bombing of her house. She saw the entire scene from the other end of the street and never really recovered from the loss of her loved ones. As was the usual case, the woman, wholly dependent on her husband for support, fell into very bad times, having been forced to vacate what was left of her house and sell most of her possessions. Hers was a story of many women during that long bloody war and their loneliness, suffering and poverty were to last throughout their lives.

Chapter 12

A city's war

Olive divided her time between her bed and the pub and leaned on her eldest daughter even more heavily over the following months. Francis was working shifts in the café and doing what she could to oversee the rest of the family. She was nearing exhaustion having just finished the breakfast shift in the café and froze when the Prime Minister's announcement of war came over the radio. The entire clientele were silenced by the crackling words of Neville Chamberlain as he spoke to the nation. War had been expected and now it was upon them. It had been hoped that it could be averted, even though, as a precautionary measure, evacuation of the children had begun shortly before the announcement. A migration to the country also took place of people leaving their homes to seek safer accommodation away from the pending war.

Francis occupied a large room at the top of the house her mother was currently renting. There were many large, elaborately furnished Victorian houses standing empty, those that could be rented out were, the rest virtually abandoned by those owners who had left them for safer climes until all danger of war had passed. It was Olive's practice to rent such houses, strip them of any furnishings that were sellable and finally, when no rent was paid, ingratiate herself by weaving an elaborate tale to the landlord gaining another few months' grace before the family were finally turned out onto the street. Nothing ever changed and Francis carried the shame and persecution on her shoulders every day, causing her to be a withdrawn and sullen young woman, with good reason.

The current family house was a three-story with a large number of bedrooms, dearly needed for the five sisters and brother. Their mother was rarely there and while their father had worked for the British Railway, he also worked a garden allotment. This was a small plot of land dedicated to his use to grow vegetables, berries and anything else that was edible, without which they would probably have starved in the early years. Victor had been born in one of the little cottages surrounding the allotments and was well versed in the ways of the land and the growing of food for survival. What a thrill it was for the youngsters to troop down to the allotment and harvest the vegetables and fruits. They could hardly wait to get them home, particularly the berries, although in the case of the huge gooseberries, very few made it home, as each child would cram as many in their mouths as would fit, gurgling with pleasure. Their father would store the freshly dug potatoes in sacks to be saved in a dark place for food during the winter months; the kids were always excited when they were given a couple of empty sacks. They would rush around gathering the autumn leaves and stuffing the sacks to make an effigy of Guy Fawkes for Bon Fire night.

Francis always relayed the story of Guy Fawkes each November 5th. The night always followed the same pattern. As soon as their sister began the tale of the unfortunate Brit, the kids would immediately stop their celebratory preparations, plonk themselves down on the floor at her feet, all straight-faced, with eyes riveted on her.

"Guy Fawkes was a villain, you know," she would say very gravely. "He was a Briton who had tried to blow up the Houses of Parliament in 1605 hoping to murder King James the first and his Ministers so that the Catholics could rule the country, but somebody told on him and his gang and 'let the cat out of the bag' about their deadly plan. They got nicked and were all caught and executed. Thereafter every year on November 5th, the residents of every little village and town construct a huge bonfire and burn a Guy Fawkes model."

The children never got tired of hearing the story; their favourite part of the ceremony was when everybody baked potatoes in their jackets in the embers of the fire and good times were had by all.

Francis always remembered those days and how her father tried to manage with no support from her mother. She always made allowances for him, knowing his limitations. He was a weak, undisciplined man, governed by his masculine instincts, unable to make a decision, certainly incapable of influencing his rebellious wife who, true to form was always off following her own pursuits, her only contribution being to bring every stray cat which took her fancy into the home, most of which were not house trained; just one more little chore waiting for Francis when she got home. There were too many mouths to feed by that time and it was practically impossible to keep up with cats as well. Times were particularly bad as her father was now full time in the Navy and no longer worked for the railway or managed the allotment which meant even less food to put on the table.

With the onset of war and the need for blackout at night, Guy Fawkes's day was abandoned. The kids were bitterly disappointed but young and old realised the urgency of the situation. Christmas too during wartime was very different for most people but to Francis and her siblings it was much the same as it always had been with little of anything. The government had issued ration books to everybody to make sure there was a fair allotment of food. National Registration Day took place in the autumn of 1939 and after each family had registered the number of occupants in the house they were issued their books in 1940. The books were produced in different colours, depending on whether for adults or children or pregnant women and entitled them to different products according to their needs.

Even though the value of the ration books was doubled on some items during the festive season, the family still struggled as by the time Francis received the coupons from her mother they were sadly depleted She was determined; however, that her brother and sisters would have some kind of joy over the season. She would put them to work making paper chains to hang about the room and then send them off to gather holly. The old lady down the road had a magnificent holly tree in her garden always loaded with berries which were hard to find. Mrs. Wilson had allowed the children to take a few branches so they didn't have to make red wax berries and stick them on the boughs. As they rushed out, Francis issued strict instructions. "Now you be careful, don't just grab what you want, knock on the door and get Mrs. Wilson's permission again. Watch your manners we don't want to upset the old lady." They would burst through the door some time later laden with holly which would be strewn around the room in strategic spots. Her gifts to them on Christmas morning were always something edible, usually an apple and/or orange with a few nuts which she would stuff into old socks and hang on each child's bedpost making sure the nuts didn't fall through the inevitable holes. It always made her smile when she thought of their faces so happy with their meagre presents

Easter time was still an exciting time for the kids thanks to their elder sister. Chocolate Easter eggs had disappeared but when fresh ones were available, the children still painted faces with neckties or necklaces on them and arranged them in baskets with straw. The winner of the best looking arrangement received a little treat of an apple or whatever Francis had managed to get hold of, usually fruit that had 'accidentally' fallen to the ground off the market stalls. The merchants generally turned a blind eye when they saw Francis rush to grab the 'fallers' hardly before they hit the deck; in fact one kindly fellow used to 'accidently on purpose' fall against the stall to knock some of the merchandise to the ground giving Francis a knowing wink, winning a grateful smile in return.

****

Francis had been grateful for the position in the café when it was offered to her. The proprietor was an old lady who had inherited the business following her husband's demise and ran a 'tight ship'. Francis was worked into the ground for a pittance but the old lady always saw that she was well nourished with plenty of food; she was smart enough to know that the thin waif-like girl would be of no use to her if her strength failed and she was a good willing worker, asking for nothing, just to do her job and pick up her pay.

Old May, as she was called, was aware of the girl's circumstances and knew that her only food was what she was given on the job. "That mother of hers should be shot." She muttered angrily to herself as she scrubbed the sandwich board. "One child after another and never there to look after them; all of them running wild. If it was not for Francis, they would have starved." She was aware that Francis was first in line for any 'yesterday's leftovers' that she could take home. Whenever there was anything, hardened though the old woman was, she softened her heart and tried to give the girl a bag of goodies most days when she left at the end of the day. The huge slabs of fruit cake were always a favourite. Any scraps from that were a real treat.

Francis earned her money, not only with the harsh conditions, but also with having to deal with the British Railway shift workers who meant no harm but were unintentionally crude. She learned to be personable but distant, keeping their leering looks and familiar remarks at bay while keeping them sweet, ensuring a few pence tip, albeit thrown carelessly on the table but like gold to her as her boss allowed her to keep all gratuities for herself. She had worked at the café for some months and was actually getting a few items of clothing and necessities up together. Everything had to be locked away though, as her mother would steal anything she was able to get her hands on while also relieving Francis of any cash at every opportunity. "For Fran's keep," Olive always said.

One night Francis was on her way home. It was late and she had worked in the little café since 7:00 in the morning. She pulled her scarf tighter around her frozen face; she was always cold, being so thin with no spare fat on her bones. The silent streets were devoid of any lifeform. She had a strong sense of foreboding and feeling utterly alone quickened her step. To her horror, she heard the low droning of the plane. Stiff with fear she threw herself up against an old building wall and crouched in terror. The droning came closer and drawing her body as far against the wall as possible, mesmerized in fear she saw the plane come into sight at the end of the road. It was flying so low she could easily see the pilot sitting bolt upright like a robot and the huge Swastika on the plane's side panel. The 'death machine' cruised slowly past up the street and behind the buildings further up the road. There was a colossal explosion radiating light across the sky for miles.

"Looks like the sod dropped his load," Francis gasped. "What an idiot for a navigator he was obviously sent to bomb the station and flew straight over it, thank God. Better get moving, head for the shelter."

And she ran, oh how she ran for what seemed an eternity, dodging huge chunks of shrapnel raining down in a never-ending stream of molten metal fanning out in all directions. Small fires were igniting everywhere. Just a few more yards, she thought and then she was flinging herself down the steps of the shelter. Once in safety, she could not contain herself and shaking badly groped her way to one of the benches. There were a few others huddled in their misery. Francis noted with relief that somebody had thought to get Lyza out of her house and brought to safety. The old lady was so frail and ailing but managed a weak smile when she saw Francis, who immediately sat down close to her, both sharing what warmth they had left in their bodies. The shelters were not built for comfort and the cold penetrated every pore. This was a communal structure but many people had built Andersen Shelters in their back gardens, they were made of corrugated steel, half buried and covered with earth. They were damp as they invariably flooded with the rains. The government assisted the poor with funding for these shelters, while there was a reasonable cost for the more well to do. Another type of construction, the Morrison Shelter also afforded some indoor protection from the incessant onslaught of bombs.

Fortunately, the old lady soon dozed off and Francis suddenly overcome with exhaustion closed her eyes thinking of the plane again and how low it had flown. Thank God he didn't drop any gas bombs. She was furious with herself for forgetting to carry the little box with the strap in which a gasmask was housed. The government were issuing gas masks because of the threat of poisoned gases being developed by the Germans for them to drop from the air. I would have been a 'gonna', she shuddered at the thought. Forcing herself to think about something more positive, she recalled the night she had first met Hamish.

****

Returning home from work one evening and after ploughing through the usual horrors of cleaning up after the cats, Francis braced herself for the job of tackling the kitchen. There was very little food in the cupboard, what on earth was she going to give the kids for dinner? There were some potatoes left, but what would she put with them? She noted with rage there was hardly any milk left either, black tea again for her; had to save what milk there was for the kids. She could see another impending scene with her mother. No doubt she'd get the usual explanatory verbiage as to why there was never any food in the cupboard. Francis had nothing to work with and was sick to her stomach of looking into the hungry, pinched faces of her brother and sisters. Her eye fell on the brown paper bag Old May had given her and she seized upon it. Overcome with joy, she pulled out a tin of corned beef and immediately started peeling the potatoes with renewed vigour.

****

Looking at the tin of corned beef, Francis remembered the fearful row which ensued recently when she had confronted her mother who was selling the coupons in the ration books to others. Even whole pages were torn from the books and sold to other people to place in their own books; a very lucrative scam for Olive, profiteering once again at the family's expense. Francis soon realized that little could be gained from the rationing and they would still be 'scratching' for food.

They still shopped at Joe's grocery store. He had managed to keep it going as long as he could after the death of his wife Mary but his heart wasn't in it anymore and he, too, passed away shortly thereafter. Mary had been his world and when she was gone, it was as if the light had been turned off in his life. Upon his passing, the shop was taken over by his remaining son and young family.

Francis thought about dear Joe and the family for a while and the fact that Joe and later his son had always extended credit to them, even turning a blind eye when they couldn't make the payments. Their kindness had made the difference between eating or not on many occasions. She would be eternally grateful for their compassion and whenever she could get hold of coupons, she would certainly give Joe's boy the business; however small. Little did she know that food rationing in Britain was to be ongoing until the mid-1950s and many would continue to go hungry.

****

Having prepared the corned beef and potato fritters Francis called up the stairs, "Come on kids, dinner's up." There was a stampede of footsteps as they all herded into the kitchen. "Get to the sink and wash your hands while there's a bit of hot water left," she yelled, obsessive as always about bodily cleanliness. She knew that the utilities were due to be shut off again because as usual the electricity bill had not been paid. Her numerous reminders to her mother had fallen on barren ground. It filled Francis with anger because she knew she contributed more money than her share to the family funds but her mother would always whine, "I'm a bit short this month luv, could you help out? I'll see you all right next week." Of course Olive never honoured her obligations. Any cash went straight back into the pub or gambling or whatever else she was in to. Wanda and Maude each had little jobs which brought in a few shillings but there were so many areas to cover that they all went short.

Francis slapped a large portion on each plate in front of each child and a lull settled in the kitchen while all eagerly devoured their food.

"Now, close your eyes, we've got a real treat coming up."

Old May had been especially generous and had hacked off a large brick of the rich fruit cake. Francis put a lavish slice in front of each child.

"OK open up," she giggled.

"Oh jumping Jupiter," cried Dugan, and, "Oh boy oh boy!"

Francis then put a generous amount of milk in their hot tea and served each.

"Now get that down you and don't waste a drop, there's good milk in there."

Much later when the kids had dispersed, she was still at the sink wrinkling her nose at the putrid black tea which she sipped occasionally. She wondered if she would hold out long enough to get the young'uns washed and herself ready for bed. She heard the front door go and her father's voice talking to somebody.

"Who in God's name has he brought in tonight?" she muttered. "Never mind visitors, it would be really nice to get some provisions in for a change."

Her father appeared beaming all over his face accompanied by a very shy young man dressed in the uniform of the Royal Air Force. Francis was dumbfounded. She stared openly and simply could not take her eyes off the young man. What on earth was her father doing bringing him to this hovel and suddenly aware of her appearance and covered with confusion, she rushed past them spluttering, "Please excuse me, I'll be back shortly." Hurling herself upstairs, her eyes smarting for she never cried, in fact she often wondered if she would ever be able to cry again. How could he do this, she thought furiously, bringing a young chap like that here with me looking like this? Viciously she tore a comb through her thick black curly hair, ripping some out in her fury, splashed some water on her face and reached for her one and only lipstick, hidden at the back of the cupboard, lest her mother should get her hands on it. Finding her prized possession still in its place, with a sigh of relief, she dabbed a little colour on her lips. Thinking there wasn't much of an improvement she made her way back downstairs again.

Her father had found two beers at the back of the cupboard and managed to find two glasses. Francis was glad to see he kept the chipped one for himself and gave the only decent one to the young man.

"And here's to my daughter Francis," Victor proudly announced, raising his glass and, "Fran, this is Hamish, he's from Scotland you know and is serving in the Royal Air Force. We met up in the local and got together to share a pint."

"That's nice," stammered Francis, "Pleased to meet you and what have you brought in the bag, Dad?"

"Help yourself, girl," her father said grandly as if by feeding his family he was doing them a favour.

Francis noted the goodies with satisfaction, tea, chocolate, biscuits, bread even a little jam, leftovers from the Navy Mess which her father had been able to sneak out. She was aware the young man was looking at her intently as she put the items in the cupboard and consumed with embarrassment managed to keep her back to them while she busied herself at the sink.

"Well, it was very nice meeting you, Hamish; I have to get the kids ready for bed now." She wiped her hands and extended one in friendship. Hamish eagerly took it and held on a little longer than was necessary. Averting her gaze she withdrew and made a hurried exit.

"So what did you think of the lad?" her father asked her later that night.

"He's too good for the likes of us," she said impatiently. "I'm surprised you brought him back here, goodness knows what he thought about this place."

"Oh he wasn't interested in the place, doubt if he even noticed it," her father retorted knowingly, beaming all over his face. "In fact, I think he was smitten with you all right. Oh yes, even asked if he might come again and maybe chat with you."

"He never did," she almost screamed. "You're just making it up to get a rise out of me."

"No honestly. Young Hamish wants to see more of you, you mark my words. I'll invite him round for a bite to eat next time."

"Well you or Mum had better make sure there's something to feed him with, that's all I can say," she retorted angrily.

Later that night in her room she wondered what the young serviceman could possibly see in her. She decided to put the whole matter out of her head. Her father had a vivid imagination and had misconstrued the situation.

She prepared herself for bed, found a long pair of socks, full of holes but nevertheless fairly warm, pulled up the thin worn blanket and then laid her old coat on top. Settling down she realized how weary she was, every bone in her body ached. She would have another really early start in the morning to get to the café. Another long week she thought and I'll be putting in extra hours over the weekend.

****

She wasn't sure how long she had slept not having a watch but awoke stiff and frozen. People had started to move about outside the shelter, putting out fires and clearing debris. "Come let's go Auntie Lyza, time to get you home," she said. The old lady stirred and managing a brief smile struggled to her feet.

Much later, having settled Lyza in her own home, Francis started the trek home. I wonder how the kids got on, she thought anxiously. She never knew what she was going to find when confusion hit and more and more bombs were being dropped on the town.

"Please, please let them be all right," she wailed as she quickened her step.

Workers were being enlisted for the factories. She knew she would be taken and although the hours were long, she would make more money and I'll feel a bit better about myself, she thought. I'll be helping the war effort, making parachutes for our boys. She knew she would also be doing her bit for the war effort with Dugan over the weekend. They had been conscripted, along with many other youth to work in volunteer groups, assigned various duties by the government for the war effort. The two, along with others, would be surveying the area for any fires that might be occurring. There were many volunteer groups such as the Royal

Observer Corps, formed with people from diverse walks of life. They were men and women volunteers who monitored the skies for enemy aircraft and reported sounds or sightings to control centres and of course the British Red Cross and Order of St. John known as Voluntary Aid Detachments in aid of the sick and wounded. The Government cancelled all National holidays in aid of the war effort and recruited every available person into needy positions.

The bombing was major during the first few years of the war in particular 1940 and 1941. The Southampton Blitz, as it was called, devastated the town. The Luftwaffe (German Air force) bombarded the streets with machine gun fire, even though the docks were the main target. These assaults left over 600 civilians dead and over 1,000 wounded, many seriously. The massive burning of the town lit up the sky and could be seen across the channel as far as France.

All of these horrors bounced back and forth in Francis's head as she made her way home that night.

****

Arriving for work the following morning, Francis saw that some of the early shift workers from the railway were seated at the end table. One of the group was addressing the others. His voice cracked with emotion as he relayed the horror of the bombing of the Civic Centre. “Bloody Germans,” he shrieked, dropped more than 10 bombs in one day on the town. One plane just dumped over 500 pounds of explosives on a school.” He paused to bury his face in his handkerchief. “Those poor little kids,” he said over and over again. “Never had a chance. Murdered.” Prostrate with grief, the man pushed back his chair and said gruffly, “Sorry blokes, I’ll see you back at the station.” After his hasty exit the rest of the group sat in silent contemplation. Francis noted their plates were still full, their food untouched when they left, so sick at heart were they.

Chapter 13

Wanda departs

Olive spent more and more time in the pub to the point that she was almost living there. Sam had long since gone and the couple that ran the establishment were very good to her. She drew the crowd and they were grateful for the business. Olive never missed an opportunity to 'lose' a few pounds from the cash till and although never caught in the act; it eventually became obvious to the proprietors that she was not to be trusted as the losses reached alarming proportions. Olive was completely indignant and filled with rage when they finally showed her the door. "You've done your business no good, no good at all. People will soon get to know how you've treated me. You're going to regret this." She screamed in fury as she flounced out.

It wasn't long before Olive found another pub close to the docks where she was able to ply her trade and earn a few pounds playing for the 'dockies' who frequented the bar. There was a hard core of Irish navies who had crossed the Channel looking for work and found themselves in the shipyards. Olive was strongly attracted to these rebels and acquired a very convincing Irish accent which she turned to her advantage at every opportunity. She also had a very lucrative business going on the side due to the high percentage of goods which went missing during the loading and unloading of the ships. It was impossible for the authorities to keep up with the huge losses and abate the black marketing and racketeering which was prolific particularly during these hard times.

One day having been away from the house all day, Olive appeared wearing a Women's Auxiliary Forces (WAF) uniform.

"What's going on, Mum?" Francis demanded.

"Well your mum is a fully fledged WAF member now, aren't you proud?" Olive cavorted around the kitchen showing off her uniform.

"But, Mum, what about all the kids? How are they going to manage if you're away all the time?"

"Wanda's been living at her boyfriend's place most of the time and with her job in the department store, she'll be all right. Dugan is big boy now and can take care of himself and now that Maude is working at the grocery store she's all right as well. You'll be around to oversee Belinda and Davina when I'm not here so what's the problem? Anyway, there's no point in giving me grief, Fran, my mind is set and the arrangements have all been made."

Olive watched her eldest daughter rush angrily from the room. Oh how selfish they are, she thought, don't I get a chance to do what I want to for a change. They'll manage. I don't know what all the fuss is about.

In the early 1940s many young unmarried women had been conscripted. Olive was among the many married women who joined the forces. Some worked in factories building aircraft or munitions; others served on RAF bases holding down a variety of driving positions. Olive was really enjoying life as she had managed to land herself a plumb job driving a staff car. The car gave her all the freedom she needed to follow her own activities and pursuits which she did at every opportunity and when Victor had told her that he had been called up from the Naval Reserve to serve full time in the Navy she was absolutely thrilled.

"That's great news, luv; more money for the kids that'll get us on our feet."

Olive was actually doing quite well herself as the weeks progressed. She was getting established in the WAF and collecting an allowance for living on camp while spending most of her time out of the service quarters. Even with the extra money, she was always behind in the rent.

Over the following months her newfound freedom under the guise of a career accelerated Olive's dislike for her husband which bordered on hatred and she continued to please herself. They rarely saw each other as Victor also lived on the service base. Olive had made arrangements for a healthy allotment from his salary to be deposited into the bank for her 'family' needs, although the family saw very little in the way of improvement. Every time she wanted the allowance upgraded, she'd whine petulantly "Vic you know you've left me with a full load here to manage. I need every pound I can get to keep our heads above water."

As her father was also now based in quarters, it fell to Francis to keep things going.

Thank goodness our Fran is around, Olive thought. Of course kids should be supportive of the family and she's old enough to know the score now. It's a pity that Wanda is such a self-opinionated young woman. Won't get her hands dirty or help in any way; always round at that boyfriend's house. I'll have to do something about that. His parents are going to wonder if the girl's got a home of her own.

****

Francis was at the kitchen sink clearing the usual heap of dirty dishes which always seemed to be waiting for her. She jumped violently at the sound of her mother bursting in with her latest man friend. Pushing him into the room Olive said, "Won't be a minute, darlin', just want to freshen up."

The man stared insolently at Francis and slowly advanced across the kitchen. In absolute horror she recoiled behind the end of the table, but still he advanced. Gathering every ounce of strength, she pushed past him and rushed up the stairs, making it to her bedroom by a slim margin. Hurling her door shut on the degenerate, she pushed the chair under the door handle to jam it closed.

A few minutes later Olive's voice rang out, "Oh there you are, darling. Came to find me did you? Just couldn't wait another minute could you?"

Francis, almost sick with disgust, sank wearily on the edge of the bed. This incident had not been the first and she wondered how long she would be able to ward off these awful men her mother kept bringing to the house. "I've got to make myself safe somehow," she whispered to herself. "I've got to stop her somehow. She's managed to wreck all our lives so far."

She recalled the day she had come home and found Dugan bawling his eyes out. He had walked in on his mother and her latest beau. He had been in a state of hysteria, blurting out, “She’s always ‘at it’ with some bloke or another. How can she treat dad like this? Doesn’t she care about him at all?” Francis had tried to comfort him but he was inconsolable, screaming, “I’m getting out of here. As soon as I’m old enough I’m going to join the Navy. I’ll get away from her if it’s the last thing I do.”

The situation went from bad to worse. Olive had become out of control.

One day Wanda had come back from Leo’s to get her belongings. “I’m moving out,” she told Francis. “I’m not putting up with her anymore. Every time I start to get on my feet she steals my stuff and whenever I do manage to get a decent boyfriend, she’s right there to destroy any chance I have to better myself. I can be saying goodnight to a friend and there’s Mum and Dad, when he’s in town, rolling up to the door drunk and stoned out of their minds, him relieving himself against the door post and her screaming obscenities. No Franny, I’ve got to go I can’t lose Leo as well. I’m sick of seeing Dugan die a little more each day with the shame she’s bringing to this house and just look at Belinda what a hopeless wreck she is. Fancy having your nerves shot to pieces when you’re her age. She’s terrified of everything and everybody, particularly mum who I’m going to end up killing if Davina doesn’t beat me to it. No, I’ve had enough; I can’t stand any more misery. I just have to go.” With that, she rushed to her room.

A short while later she appeared with a small bag of belongings. “I’m going to Leo’s place. His mum said I could stay there and with the few pounds I’m earning at the department store I should be able to get on my feet.” She was crying. “Franny I’m so sorry, I don’t want to leave you, but it’s everyone for themselves. If you’re smart you’ll get as far away from her as you can.”

Francis felt sorry for her younger sister. She knew her mother would make things hot for her and sure enough, a few days later Wanda was dragged back, basically by the scruff of her neck. A bruise was beginning to manifest itself on her face where Olive had shown her the back of her hand. The girl was screaming obscenities at her mother and struggling to free herself from the vice like grip. Francis helped her upstairs and Wanda flung herself hysterically on the bed, beating it with her fists until exhausted, she lay quietly staring at the ceiling.

Francis sat down next to her hardly able to get her thoughts together. “Wanda,” she spoke carefully, “I’ll fix it with mum so that she’ll have to let you go and then I’m going to speak to Leo’s mother to make sure she is prepared to have you live with them.

“Oh, Franny, would you do that for me? God bless you.” Wanda grabbed her sister’s hand and held it so tightly Francis thought she’d break her fingers; she spoke grimly.

"Just leave it with me for a couple of days. I'll get you free of this.

Francis waited for her mother to come home alone and the opportunity presented itself the next day.

"Oh there you are, Fran." Olive spoke airily. "And what's little madam up to? Has she been into work today? She'd better have, she owes me something for her keep."

"Well, Mum," Francis said defiantly. "I'm glad you brought up the subject of Wanda because I'm going to make you a proposition. You're going to let her go and get on with her life. You'll not interfere with her in any way or disgrace yourself in front of Leo's family and here's why. You make one move towards her and dad is going to hear about your goings on. Furthermore, I think the WAF Administration might want a little insight into your activities."

Olive's normally sallow complexion turned bright red with rage. "How dare you, you ungrateful, pathetic little creature. Who do you think you are threatening your mother?" she screamed.

Unyieldingly, Francis held her ground and demanded, "What's your answer, Mum? Does she go or am I opening my mouth?"

"The little madam can go and good riddance," Olive blazed, privately thinking Francis could go with her, but she needed her so she said nothing more, except, "Get her out of this house. I don't want to set eyes on the selfish stuck-up little brat again."

Francis went and put her coat on struggling to fasten the buttons, her hands were shaking so badly. She brushed her black unruly curls and finally succeeded in making herself marginally presentable. Her head ached and felt like a ton weight on her shoulders but she walked briskly with confidence to meet with Leo's mother. Sometime later, sitting in the little parlour, she put up a good argument for Wanda.

"She's a good girl really, hard-working, industrious and determined to make something of herself. She has a nice little job and will be able to help out with a few pounds and a little housework." Leo's mother beamed.

"We like the girl Francis you don't have to sell her. All she needs is a chance away from that mother of yours and Leo thinks the world of her. Francis stood up.

"I'll go and help her get her stuff together and bring her down to your place. You won't regret it."

Leo's mother patted Francis's shoulder.

"I know she'll be all right it's you I'm worried about. How will you manage?"

"I can take care of myself, thanks." Francis said defensively and started towards the door.

Wanda was elated when Francis gave her the news. "Get your stuff together. I'm taking you to Leo's. Come on get a move on before mum gets in. I don't want any more trouble."

Francis and Wanda arrived at Leo's home, breathless with the exertion of the packing and carrying bags down the road. Wanda turned and Francis was shocked at the hatred on her younger sister's face.

"I detest that so called mother of ours. I swear she'll never be a part of my life again." Wanda was as good as her word; she carried the hatred with her for the rest of her life.

Chapter 14

Marriage

The two sat huddled on the railway embankment under the bridge. He held her hand tightly and with great formality, noting the seriousness of the occasion, Hamish asked Francis to marry him. She accepted and he kissed her. Neither was big on ceremony but never had she felt such happiness. She knew she would never be loved by anyone as this young man loved her and she reciprocated as much as she was able. Their partnership, she vowed, would be for life. Security at last, she thought, finally a proper home of my own. Later, fishing a bag of toffees out of his pocket, he handed them to her saying in all earnest, "Just to mark the occasion Fran," and both howled with laughter so hard they almost fell down the embankment.

They were married on February 14, 1942, Valentine's Day, the day for lovers to affirm their vows.

****

Francis remained at the house after she married. Her new husband was based in Royal Air Force quarters, but no provision was made for his young wife, as was the case of many young service women. She had secured a job in the parachute factory. The hours were long but the pay was good compared to what she had been receiving at the little café.

When her first child was expected, Hamish thought his wife and baby would be safer up in Scotland away from the bombing and atrocities being inflicted on the City. Francis thought she was going to a new life, but the hardship was worse, compounded by the freezing damp weather. Her in-laws lived in a remote village in the Scottish Highlands surrounded by mountains and beautiful lakes which never warmed up because of a very brief summer and generally bitter cold rainy weather the rest of the year. She could never get warm and huddled for hours by the old stove with the even older family members.

Hamish's mother had died in childbirth and he was brought up by his mother's sister who, being unmarried, was glad to be provided for as a nanny and housekeeper. His father was a man of few words, kindly, but totally involved in his crops and between tending them and studying his bible, he was not very communicative. Hamish didn't talk much about his estranged elder sister, as he had been very young when she left Scotland for Australia and he barely knew her. His youngest brother Angus lived in the family home; a poor unfortunate individual with hunched back and clubbed foot. Francis was shocked when she first saw him but discovered as she spent more time with him that he was a sensitive caring young man that life had dealt all the wrong cards.

Hamish's two older brothers appeared periodically which livened up the old house a bit and she came to look forward to their visits. The pair always made her laugh when they recounted Hamish's antics as a young boy. He was good at providing food for the table and always carried a ferret in his pocket to send down the rabbit warrens and flush them out. Hamish would position himself and sack at the ready and it was a rare occasion that he didn't take something home for the pot. The brothers' favourite yarn was when Hamish had managed to get himself a little job after school as the train gatekeeper. It was his responsibility to change the position of the tracks enabling the train to pass through into the village. Unfortunately he always had his nose in a book and invariably failed to throw the switch because he didn't hear the whistle of the oncoming train. The train was re-routed on several occasions. That always brought a smile to the faces of the villagers not having much excitement in their lives. When Hamish entered the RAF his trips to Scotland were few and far between and his brothers saw little of him. Starved for news of any sort, they were always keen to hear about life down south and being a serviceman. Their guffaws and riotous laughter brightened up the dingy little sitting room especially when Hamish told them that nobody could understand the Gaelic and he was having speech training classes to learn the 'English language'.

The family had a barrel of smoked herrings at the back of the house and potatoes stored in sacks buried in the soft damp earth within the shed. Francis would never forget the tasty powdery potatoes set up in a huge casserole dish in the centre of the table with a brick of butter to go with them. Her mouth watered just at the thought of them; they tasted even better than her dad's from the allotment. Must have been something to do with the soil, she decided. Then there were the peas piled high in their basket. What a pleasure shelling them. The family would draw on these foods which were their main diet supplemented by the odd chicken and rabbit. She had been horrified the first time she heard the rumpus outside and rushing to the tiny window saw Hamish's aunt chasing the old rooster round the yard with a chopper. What a sight, the old lady's skirts billowing out in the wind and the chopper hurling through the air. She had never been able to catch it apparently. One night they were all sat down to dinner and the old man, Hamish's father, commented, "Ahi, that's a tough one, you finally got eem then." The old lady grinned revealing her toothless gums and Francis thought she was going to vomit all over the table.

Her despondency was heightened by the stark little cottage with its dour inhabitants. Francis found them very forbidding and always felt as if she was being watched. A young girl thrown in amongst all those old people so slow and precise in everything they did and on top of everything else she was hardly able to understand what they were saying in their broad highland dialect. Francis had to admit, though, that when her time came they certainly 'set the heather on fire' and got a move on, having her dispatched immediately to the local hospital, which was great because the primitive facilities at the cottage left a lot to be desired. The sisters who served in the local hospital where Francis had her baby were equally hard to understand, although she was never to forget the way they rallied round to help her, as she was so sick and weak. She could hear them commenting on her lack of stamina and thin, undernourished body and was eternally grateful for the care and compassion they extended. During her stay she had been able to get her hands on an old plant book and became quite an authority on the heathers which abounded throughout Scotland. In the weeks that followed she admired the Scottish heath of the genus Erica. Its inchoate buds were already encasing the stems and in December these plants would relieve the desolate moors and paint the mountains with beautiful white and pink bells, their delicate woodsy aromas pervading the air through the dreary months until spring. Francis was in awe and decided to name her first child Erica after the heath.

Following the birth of her daughter, all she could think about was getting back south where she belonged in spite of the war which raged on stronger with every day. Angus loved the babe and would spend hours just sitting looking at her. Finally, one day, Francis was tidying up the room and suddenly couldn't stand another minute of being there.

"Angus I'm going out for a while, will you watch the babe for me please?"

Angus smiled gleefully. "I'll look after the wee bairn," he said as Francis packed up all the child's belongings and her own few meagre accessories and stuffed them into a couple of bags. She hurried down to the little train station. The ticket collector in the booth looked at her with curiosity.

"Now what can I do for you, lassie?" He enquired.

"I have to get back to Hampshire. Do I have to change at Inverness and can I pay for the full trip now?"

He smiled kindly at the volley of questions she posed. "That you can, there's a train going out before noon today with a good connection."

Francis handed over her roll of money and the man pushed a few notes back in her hand. That being done she felt much better as she headed up the hill back to the house. I have a couple of hours to get myself together, she thought, feed the baby and get on my way.

****

The young woman was cold and near collapse with sheer exhaustion when she finally reached the house.

"Oh my God, it's our Fran." Maude shrieked, as she rushed to get her brother. "Fran's home, Fran's home," she kept shrieking, "we'll be all right now."

Dugan came running down the stairs two at a time and grabbed his sister enthusiastically. The baby started crying.

"Is there any milk in the house?" Francis said wearily. "It's been foul trip, I'm completely done in."

Her old room was still miraculously unoccupied, the austerity of its confines unchanged. That night Francis climbed gratefully into the old bed, having laid the infant in the old crib and dropped into a coma like state of unconsciousness.

Francis settled down to the daily grind of looking after a small baby with not much of anything. Whenever she could get hold of some wool she would calm herself by knitting little jackets, blankets, anything the babe needed, who, thank goodness, rarely cried; a lovely infant and so quiet no one would have known she was there.

She took to going to see Aunt Lyza with her daughter. She always treated the visits as special occasions, giving her the opportunity to dress the baby up in her newly knitted clothes; every item clean and freshly washed. She felt the same pride as her mother had before her when they went to visit Lyza. The child had shocking red hair like her father and beautiful blue, green eyes. What a perfect little girl. Francis was gratified every time somebody stopped and peered into the pram to admire her. Lyza was enraptured and looked forward to the visits more and more.

One day Francis arrived at the house and Lyza's lady lodger opened the door.

"I know it's not my place," she blurted out, "but I'm sick of seeing this place stripped every time one of Lyza's so-called family comes here."

Francis was mortified, knowing her mother had been up to her tricks again. Every time she went near Lyza she was robbing the old lady of all her possessions. Anything she could get her hands on disappeared, all the jewellery, ornaments, cushions, anything that she could pawn. Francis never forgot the look of accusation on the lodger's face. That was the last time she went to the house. The journey back home that day seemed unending and finally sitting in the kitchen with a cup of tea, Francis almost cried with relief, but closed her eyes tightly against the incipient tears which threatened to weaken and overwhelm her. It seemed that she had carried her mother's shame on her shoulders her entire life and how her body ached in shear weariness of the burden.

Francis's daily walk generally took her to an area referred to as 'below Bar' namely The Bargate. The Bargate, built by the Normans, was the gated entrance to the old original walled City. The most historic part of the town, below the Bargate, was virtually annihilated. The area had been bombed relentlessly until every building endured its effect. Most of the Georgian architecture and other amounting to over 40,000 buildings were lost forever. Francis didn't know why she continued to come but was drawn like a magnet. She'd sit in the ruins and survey the bleak scene. An old man was always quietly sitting there also, never speaking. Maybe he had lived there. Maybe he had lost a loved one. Francis saw him often sitting just staring, lost in another time. Maybe she should have imposed on his solitude, offered a few kind words and possibly eased his suffering in some way but at the time never felt the inclination to intrude.

Once in a while Francis would see a polish woman who had been temporarily housed in the refugee camp in the neighbourhood and was shocked to silence when Helena recounted her life. Her husband had been a great academic scholar and taught several languages and they had been well placed. Following the invasion of their country, they had walked most of the way through Europe with Helena carrying her baby on her back. Francis saw the fear manifested on her friend's face as she talked of their escape to France and subsequent fleeing when that country too was invaded and their final arrival in England. The memories of torture and abuse of the polish and polish Jews and the deaths of those who had befriended them, were constantly to the fore, consequently, her husband became a serious liability for Helena being prone to fits and horrendous depression. Following the war they were placed in permanent housing and became British citizens, nevertheless the trauma of earlier years was always to remain. Francis knew she should have shown her friend a little more empathy but her own mental state was so low with chronic depression proving an ongoing battle to overcome throughout her life and as with the old man in the ruins, she just couldn't reach out.

****

One day Dugan came in smiling all over his face. "Well I've gone and done it," he said, slapping Francis on the back. “I’ve joined the Navy; I’m shipping out next week.” Francis was horrified and Dugan, seeing her stricken face said, “Common, Fran, be happy for me, I’m a big lad now, it’s time I made my own way. Besides,” he added, when I’ve made enough money, Ellie and me is gonna get married.” He gave her a reassuring hug.

“Is there any grub around, I’m starving?”

“There’s a bit of bread and cheese in the cupboard, not much of anything else I’m afraid.”

The house seemed deathly quiet in the weeks that followed. Dugan was a lively boy and his leaving weighed heavily on Francis. He was sadly missed.

****

When Francis realised she was expecting another baby she was filled with despair. She was so young, undernourished and desperately poor. Here we go again, she thought angrily. How will we ever manage, we barely have enough to survive on now? She was distraught with insecurity and filled with resentment. The financial situation had improved marginally since her marriage but there was still little money and certainly another child would prove too big a stretch for the budget.

Helena was quite a regular visitor now and Francis was glad of her friendship and began to look forward to her visits. Helena was developing a very practical approach to life, accepting the pitfalls much more passively, striving to forget the past and focussing more on the future; commendable considering the desperate times they were living in. The pair would congregate in the kitchen and Helena would make a pot of borscht, her traditional beetroot soup. She'd put rice, potatoes or homemade dumplings with the beetroot, whatever was available. If there was any bread in the cupboard, Francis would hack off a couple of chunks for dipping. How both enjoyed these times and oh what a feast.

Helena was always asking after Hamish.

"I hope you realize how lucky you are to have a husband like him."

She'd repeat herself over and over again finally succeeding in pulling Francis out of the doldrums for a while, making her appreciate the wonderful virtues of her young husband.

Hamish had done very well in the RAF being highly motivated to become a pilot as his keen interest in aircraft developed. The Germans had developed the first jet plant powered by liquid fuel to be used in combat which was utilized in the war in 1944. Their pride was boundless when the plane, the Messerschmitt, nicknamed Willy after its developer, Wilhelm, set the world speed record. Hamish was promoted eventually to Flt. Lieutenant; however he was assigned as a navigator and to his ongoing regret was never able to fulfil his dream of becoming a pilot.

Chapter 15

WW2 ends

Francis was making her tea in the kitchen when Olive put in one of her rare visits.

"I'm having Belinda and Davina evacuated." Olive stated in an offhand manner.

"No you will not." Francis screamed, banging her fist on the table. "Dad will have something to say about that."

"Dad is away doing his bit for the war effort, you know that, Fran, and anyway it's not like they're going far. I'm not shipping them overseas, what kind of mother do you think I am?" Olive whined petulantly. Her daughter scowled.

"Don't look at me like that, Fran," Olive shrieked. Francis was rigid with tension. She knew that her mother had no interest in the family and over 2,500 children had already been evacuated overseas.

Prior to 1940 out of the original evacuees, over one million mothers and children returned home from Canada and the United States as the expected bombing of the major cities had not taken place. Many of the original evacuees never returned to their homeland. The evacuation progression was halted in 1940 when one of the evacuation ships was torpedoed and sunk and over 70 evacuees were drowned, but the process resumed later that year.

Francis knew that while her mother spent no time or money on her family, they were still a liability of which she would like to rid herself. Needless to say, Olive had her way and a couple of days later Francis returned from work to find that Belinda and Davina were gone.

She sat at the kitchen table; head in hands, depression engulfed her totally and completely. The war had been raging since 1939 and it was now 1944. Everybody had hoped it would be over by this time especially with the aggressive intervention of the Allied Forces across Europe but the Germans had launched an all-out attack on Britain by sending missiles across the English Channel. Southampton Docks was a key target as it handled military aids for the Allies. Many children were now being sent from the south to inland cities to protect them from the onslaught and in retrospect Francis realized the two girls would be much safer.

****

The two sisters stood at the railway station forlorn and fiercely defensive; their mouths tightly closed with lips pursed. Their clothes were rags and their feet cold even with the paper stuffed in their shoes to cover the holes. Tough though they were, each shivered with fear, chilled to the bone, but not from the bitter wind which bit through their thin clothing.

"Come along, girls, let's have you then," yelled the station master, "Get a move on down the platform, the train's coming any minute."

The evacuation program was designed to ship some children out to farms in the country others to cities such as Winchester. Belinda and Davina were assigned to go to the country. They had been placed in the care of one of the farming families and were scheduled to remain there until the end of the war. They were to help out with housekeeping duties and light labouring in the fields.

The train pulled into the station with a screech of brakes and a rush of steam through a blackened funnel. The porter pushed the two girls along into an empty carriage. The two were soon joined by another group of young people. They all sat down on the benches eying each other surreptitiously. Cold and exhausted Belinda and Davina huddled together for warmth and although hungry, soon fell asleep. They were loudly awakened by the porter who hustled them off the train over to one side of the station. A large fat woman with an older man moved forward with a sheet of paper.

The man shouted out loudly. "Now each of you raise a hand when I call out your name." He called out six names; Belinda and Davina raised theirs, along with four boys. "Oh good, you look like strong lads." He addressed the group of boys. "You'll be able to put in a good day." His gaze fell on the boy called Trevor. "Ah yes," he said smiling, noting the boy's tall thin but sinewy frame. "It looks like we'll get things moving. I don't know about you two though." He pointed to Belinda and Davina. "The two of you look half starved, we're gonna have to fatten you up if we're to get anything out of you."

"Oh leave them alone, the fat woman shouted. "I'll take care of them." With that she grabbed each girl's hand and started out of the station. A huge cart with benches and a make shift canopy awaited them with an even bigger horse harnessed between the shafts up front. The two girls stared in awe at the creature, they had never seen such a huge animal and what a smell; both wrinkled their noses. The woman helped them both up the steps and into the cart to the nearest bench, leaving the four boys jostling for position on the other two benches. The man climbed up front and with a crack of his whip and a "Com'on, Rosie, let's get a move on we haven't got all day." The mare snorted and off she went at a fair clip heading towards the rolling fields bordering the train station.

The girls soon learnt that, although Nellie, the farmer's wife, was rough and ready, she had a heart of gold. "Com'on" she'd say, just before each meal. "Over to the sink and get those hands scrubbed." A big slab of carbolic soap sat on the side of the sink. After the initial shock of the heavy odour, Davina and Belinda soon got quite accustomed to it, both revelling in the feeling of being fresh and clean, a sensation new to each as they had been kept so poorly with no practiced hygiene or soap in the house for that matter.

After all of the children had scrubbed their hands thoroughly, Nellie would line them up. "Right then, get those hands out front where I can see them," she'd say firmly. Any child that didn't pass her scrutiny was immediately returned to the sink to repeat the process. Following this daily ritual, each would stand behind the benches on each side of the table and Nellie would say a little prayer, always the same one; the kids wondered if she knew any other.

"Dear God," she said reverently with bowed head. "Thank you for this good food you give everybody and make us all deserving of your generosity."

Davina and Belinda always nudged each other at this point, knowing full well they had been out tilling the ground all day to make these good foods grow. Belinda would say regularly, "God wasn't there digging all day, neither was he pulling crops hours on end. I suppose there is a God, but my body's telling me who did all the work." Belinda always nodded in agreement, she was just grateful they were getting something to eat regularly. One day Nellie overheard Davina. "You watch your mouth, young lady, or God is going to sort you out for sure."

After grace everyone sat down and silence ensued as they were all ravenous after their toils of the day.

Trevor took an instant liking to Davina. Her spirit, fearful temper and sheer tenacity intrigued him. Even though he was barely 17, he felt a strong protectiveness towards her. Behind that rebellious spirit he sensed the girl's hopelessness and acceptance of her lot and made allowance for her fierce outbursts.

She sat on the fence one sunny morning swinging her legs, chomping her way through a carrot she'd just ripped out of the ground. What a picture she made; nose covered in freckles, cheeks pink from the sun and the exertion of her vegetable picking, evidenced by the enormous basket at her side, loaded with an assortment of crops. Her eyes roving unceasingly, settled on Trevor's beaming face.

"What you staring at?" she spat at him.

He just grinned and in his usual good-natured way.

“Did you want a game of football later on?”

Davina’s face lit up,

“Oh good,” she said gleefully, forgetting her outburst and earlier unpleasantries. “Give me a chance to knock the socks off you again.”

Trevor smiled, what a great kid she is he thought, though a little feisty at times.

Life was good on the farm. The girls worked hard helping in the house and on the land. Although they were near exhaustion at the end of the day, they were always rewarded with a hearty meal and a clean bed. One day there was a rumpus outside and Nellie, wiping her hands on her apron, left the kitchen to be confronted with Maude and Wanda.

“We’ve come for our sisters to take them back home,” Wanda said insolently.

Fighting to keep control Nellie said quietly, “They’re safer here. The bombing gets worse every day in the city. It’s better that they stay here.”

Wanda swept past her as if she hadn’t spoken. “Come on, girls, get your stuff together; you’re going home.” Belinda and Davina stared in amazement. They didn’t want to go back. They had begun to enjoy their life and regular food, and were even fond of Nellie who they knew was kind and had their wellbeing at heart. Wanda was determined; however and shortly after ushered them out of the door without a ‘thank you’ or even a backward glance.

Nellie was distraught. She had grown fond of both girls and was pleased with their contribution to the daily chores. They were hard working; there certainly was no slacking off in that area. Later, while she was washing the dishes, Trevor came into the kitchen looking very forlorn. “She’s gone,” snapped Nellie. “Her sisters came and took her and Belinda back home.” Trevor turned on his heel and Nellie, softening a little, knowing how fond he was of Davina, said, “Trevor do you want a piece of fruit cake? I baked it today.” She knew it was Trevor’s favourite, but shaking his head he walked out of the house. Very unlike him to turn down cake, Nellie mused, he really misses her already.

****

What do you think you’re playing at?” screamed Olive furiously at the two girls.

Wanda screamed back. “They belong here at home and if you were anything of a mother you’d be glad to see them.”

“Well they’re going straight back in the morning, Now, as you’ve already been told get out of this house this minute before you regret it and don't come back." Olive's face was contorted in rage."

"What's going on?" Francis said appearing at the doorway. Her eyes fell on Belinda and Davina huddled together in the corner.

"Wanda's leaving," Olive shouted angrily "and the two girls are going back to the farm tomorrow."

Francis moved towards her two younger sisters. "Let's go upstairs, she said, "we'll sort your stuff out and I'll make you some tea and something to eat."

Olive was as good as her word. She formally returned the two girls the next day. Nellie had been surprised but very pleased when her neighbour, breathless with exertion, having rushed all the way from the station, told her that the two girls were there with their mother waiting to be picked up. Upon Nellie's arrival at the station, the girls whooping with joy, rushed to Rosie and gave her a good pat and clambered up into the cart. Both were elated to be going back to the farmhouse with all that good food and had not even been bothered when their mother dumped them unceremoniously at the station and climbed into the next train heading back south. Old Rosie, snorting repeatedly, glanced back over her shoulder at intervals. Nellie noticed and wondered who was more pleased the old mare or her to see the two youngsters again.

The journey back to the farm was, as always, beautiful through verdant valleys and fields with sheep and cows. The kids were enraptured with the animals, particularly the Jersey cows; beautiful golden creatures with velvety noses and huge eyes heavily hooded with thick dark lashes. Little stone cottages with thatched roofs and rambling farms filled the undulating countryside. The Norman and Saxon forerunners were evidenced by numerous squares of hedgerows cutting through the land endemic to the area.

As soon as they arrived at the house, the girls rushed upstairs to their room with their meagre belongings. They were in a hurry to get back to the kitchen and sample some of Nellie's goodies. Both were sick with hunger, as they had eaten little since leaving the farm the day before. Falling over each other, they hurled themselves downstairs and headed for the sink in the kitchen. Nellie beamed with pleasure; they certainly know the routine, she thought as each girl presented her hands for inspection. Suddenly, the door burst open and Trevor rushed in, grabbed Davina and flung her up over his back. Returning her to the tiled floor he said, "How about giving me a play-off game after dinner, if that's all right?" he said quickly to Nellie.

"Course it is," she beamed.

"Now come on all of you up to the table. I'm, dishing up now." She certainly got no argument on that score. Silence reigned except for the occasional champing all around the table. Soon all were replete of good food and the kitchen resumed its usual hub of activity.

Christmas was fast approaching and the next day when everyone was sitting at breakfast, Nellie announced that they were all going down to the church that evening for an evening service and to see the lights. The German forces were now concentrating their attacks utilizing missiles and rockets, without the use of conventional aircraft and because of this blackout regulations were lifted and the churches were again displaying their stained glass windows for the first time in four years.

Later that day the kids gathered around the old horse and cart. Nellie handed them a beautiful red harness with bells which she had lovingly stored in the attic over the years. It had originally been worn on special occasions by Rosie's mother who was descended from the huge Dutch Friesian horses brought over to England in the 16th century. The breed had been refined over the years when the organization for Shire horses was initiated but Rosie still stood 17 hands (68 inches high, which was generally the size of the Shire stallion. She was enormous.

The kids were all over poor old Rosie who didn't quite know what was going on although she soon entered into the spirit with an occasional snort of appreciation at the oos and ahhs of the young people as she was dressed up for the occasion. Nellie then followed up with an inspection of all for cleanliness and tidiness and they all climbed on board. Everybody sang carols as they jogged along. Belinda and Davina just couldn't believe their eyes when they arrived. Nellie explained that the church was hundreds of years old and constructed completely of solid stone throughout. They were flabbergasted at the stained glass windows all lit up and welcoming, but more than a little ill at ease when they entered through the great wooden arched doors, as they had never been inside a church before. God's house, my goodness, what would he think of the likes of them?

The girls were to remain on the farm for the duration of the war and did not return to the south until 1945.

****

Winston Churchill had assumed the position of Prime Minister in May 1940 and was able to deliver his great Victory speech five years later on May 8, 1945 which formalized the end of Hitler's war in Europe:

"My dear friends, this is your hour. This is not victory of a party or of any class. It's a victory of the great British nation as a whole...

The Minister continued to inflame the crowds by stating that the Great British nation had stood their ground alone against the greatest military power seen.

The people of Britain gradually picked up the remnants of their lives; each in their own ways; some reflecting on the past few years of carnage, others trying to build back some of what they had lost. Street parties abounded and more than one million Londoners celebrated the end of the war.

****

Francis's second daughter was born after the war. Those years should have been a joyous time when people were building their lives, and a time for new life but Francis still suffered through bouts of black despair and found it hard to find joy in anything. Her love of natural floribunda; however, remained. It was inherent in her as with her sister Belinda and that being so she named her second child Lily also after one of her favourite plants, the Lily of the valley, a tiny green spreading plant with rich vibrant green leaves, highly prolific displaying heavily perfumed miniature bells in May.

Her melancholy escalated one day when her mother arrived at the house with Lyza hanging frantically onto her arm. Olive was blethering on as she always did when she was being totally irrational.

"I thought if we brought Auntie Lyza back home with us it would be easier for us to take care of her," she said. Choosing to ignore Francis's horrified expression, she rambled on. "She really needs care and Fran don't give me attitude, we have plenty of room and she needs people around. Here's her bag with a few things to tide her over. I'll go back later and get the rest."

I'm sure you will, thought Francis and anything else you can get out of there.

The old lady stood quietly and realizing how weary she was, Francis stepped forward to help her to her room without another word to her mother. Helping her off with her clothes and into her nightdress, she settled her into bed. "Auntie, you have a little rest and I'll bring you a cup of tea," she said. Lyza sank down into the pillows and closed her eyes. Heading down to the kitchen, Francis wondered how she would manage to take care of her, knowing full well the only reason her mother had brought her was so that she could clear out her great aunt's house. She knew the pawnbroker would do well out of Olive's latest scheme and with Lyza's lodger now gone it would be easy for Olive to take what she wanted. Oh God, she thought, I'm already overloaded trying to keep this old house reasonably clean with two sisters, two small children and now an ailing old lady to look after as well.

As time went by Francis couldn't help comparing her two daughters; her first born, Erica, a quiet easy-going little girl and her second, Lily, the absolute opposite, wild and argumentative, always questioning everything. She found it almost impossible to hide her frustration and exhaustion dealing with a child that analysed everything and always required explanations and as the girl grew she must have sensed it. She was highly strung and would sit banging her head on the back of the chair for what seemed an eternity, almost as if she were trying to relieve her own frustrations. Francis who had been so completely deprived of affection or any form of nurturing during her growing up years, found it hard if not impossible to display any emotion and felt little warmth towards anyone, least of all her young daughter. The girl's mass of white hair was always a trial and getting the hairbrush through it was a nightmare, perhaps she was more than a little rough on occasion. No, Francis simply could not fathom her and could not grasp the fact that even though the child was so fair, she still reminded her of her mother; could it be that her temperament was so wild. Her sister on the other hand was quite a different kettle of fish, quiet and sweet, always did as she was told and never argued, a pleasure to manage.

Francis noticed that her second born had become very within herself, even withdrawn from her older sister at times. She would disappear for long periods of time but Francis knew she could be found at every opportunity with her Auntie Lyza or sitting on the garden path stroking the furry backs of the bumble bees as they slept wallowing in the warmth of the sun. Although Francis was unable to determine what her little daughter was saying, she could hear her chattering away to anything that moved, bumble bees, butterflies, birds or even the odd squirrel and occasionally shrieking at the big ginger tomcat that she had developed a positive dislike for. She would wrinkle up her nose in disgust at the smell of the animal and the fact that he always did his business by the sink in the house. Francis did manage a smile when she thought about that. The child was obsessive about cleanliness and even the slightest mark or dirt on her hands would send her running into the house in hysterics to have it cleaned off. In retrospect, Francis realised that possibly the child mimicked herself. Perhaps she was a little obsessive about personal cleanliness, she just never felt clean; almost as if she were trying to wash away the years of no soap, hot water and other essentials of which she had been so cruelly deprived.

Francis didn't try to stop the child's visits to Lyza's room. She knew the old lady derived great comfort from the little girl's incessant chatter. She wondered why her daughter never made a major issue out of the old lady's bucket placed near the bed for her to relieve herself when necessary. The bucket never seemed to get emptied and the room was rancid because nobody seemed to find the time to deal with it. The little girl would wrinkle her nose at any unpleasant odour though and would say "Oooh, Auntie's pale." This association with bad odours was to remain imbedded throughout her life.

One morning, the sisters were drinking tea in the kitchen talking about Lyza's accident. Davina being the most robust was gesticulating and talking loudly.

"My God, you should have seen the blood all over the bricks where she fell; managed to get out round to the back of the house; almost made it to the toilet and slipped right by the water barrel. You've got to admit she's a tough old bird. How she's still hanging on goodness knows; and that kid," she ranted on, "is always in that bedroom, just sitting by the bed listening to the old lady. I happened to go by the door the other day and I heard Lyza telling the girl, "In a little while a big black taxi is going to come down from the sky and it's going to take me up to heaven. Now, don't you be sad, when I'm gone because I'll always be close to you and when you feel sad or lonely, you look up at the brightest twinkling star in the sky and that will be me waving at you."

Davina paused for breath before continuing her tirade.

“I don’t think it’s right she should be filling the girl’s head with all that nonsense.”

A hush fell over the room and Francis realizing the little girl was standing in the doorway listening with a quizzical look on her face, rushed noisily forward collecting the cups and saucers and pushed them into the sink.

“Come on get over here then, let’s get your hands washed for tea.”

The child looked up at her mother and studied her face for signs of stress or anxiety. Francis always felt a little disconcerted at the child’s intent gaze. I wonder why she’s so astute, she thought, it’s almost as if she knows what people are thinking.

“So how was Auntie Lyza?” she asked abruptly.

“Well,” the little girl paused, “Auntie is waiting for the big black taxi. It’s coming soon to take her up to heaven.”

Francis was moved in spite of herself.

“That’s nice, isn’t it? Auntie’s going on a lovely holiday.”

Settling the child down in front of her tea, she said, “I think I’ll go and see if Auntie wants anything,” and deal with that wretched bucket, she thought.

Lyza opened her eyes, she felt warm and comfortable the quiescence of the room soothing her. The little girl waved from the door.

"Now who is that?" Lyza murmured. "Edward is that you? Come into the light where I can see you" and closing her eyes, she smiled in deep contentment as her dear friend held his hands out to her.

Francis sat down beside the old lady. Lyza looked so peaceful, so happy. Closing her eyes tightly and laying her hand on the little prayer book, presented to Lyza as a young woman on April 20, 1883, for the first time ever Francis prayed…

"God, if you are a true God and if in fact you even exist, here's the one thing I'm asking of you. Take this good soul and give her all the things you never thought to give her in life. She was a good person and you turned your back on her. She worked herself into the ground for others and if anyone deserves to be taken care of it's her. So do your stuff and don't let me down; that's if you're really there, of course; now's your chance to prove yourself."

She sat for a while clutching the little book tightly to her, marvelling at the sense of tranquillity and happiness radiating from the old lady's face. All signs of hard living banished from her features.

There was a small gathering up at the Old Cemetery in the Common to mark Lyza's passing and although it was a typical cold and misty morning, Lyza would have been pleased that Edward was close by. He had made arrangements prior to his passing and had managed to secure a lot in close proximity to Lyza's.

Olive put in a brief appearance. She made an impressive figure in a tightly fitting black suit enhanced by a large brimmed hat with fine mesh veil. Francis was unable to read her mother's face. Olive stood very still, her enigmatic expression set, unfathomable. Tough though she was; even Francis felt a chill run down the back of her neck.

Chapter 16

New beginnings

Maude and Belinda were giggling in the kitchen. Maude was saying, “Have you seen that Davina trying to act like a lady since Trevor started coming around? Must say he doesn’t waste much time, his ship has hardly docked and he’s here panting at the leash. Did you hear that dreadful scene with her and mum the other day? Francis had to separate them. Mum was trying to steal Davina’s silk stockings; you know the ones that Trevor had brought her when he was on leave. She was trying to get herself gussied up for Trevor to take her out when she discovered the stockings were missing. I swear to God, if it hadn’t been for our Fran, Davina would have killed mum; you should have heard them going at it.”

There was a knock at the door and Francis went to see who it was. She was confronted by a WAF officer standing there with feet firmly planted and obviously meaning business.

“Could you hold on a moment? I’ll just go and close the kitchen door, there’s a bit of a racket going on in there,” she said, a huge sense of foreboding engulfing her as she moved swiftly down the hall to close the door. Hurrying back filled with apprehension she thought she may as well get it over with and wondered what Olive had been up to this time.

“Are you Francis? You fit the description on file as being the daughter of our recruit Olive.”

Francis interrupted, the WAF officer, wishing to get the whole thing over as quickly as possible. “My mum isn’t here,” she replied defiantly.

“Do you have any idea where she is then?”

“She’s down at the pub where she always is.” Francis could have cut her tongue out, but it was too late.

“She’s supposed to be based on camp but she hasn’t been seen in days. Her ‘live-in’ allowance means just that. This is the last warning she’s getting. Just tell her to report back to the base when she gets in.”

With that the officer turned on her heel and left abruptly. Francis closed the door. Well that’s torn it, she thought. How am I going to get out of this? If she knows I’m the one that told them, she’ll kill me. “Too bad,” she said aloud and bracing her shoulders went upstairs to see to the two girls.

Later that night she heard her mother come in drunk as usual and not wanting to put it off any longer, she met Olive half way up the stairs.

"The WAF were here looking for you," she shouted. "I just told them you weren't at home. You'd better get on it in the morning, doubt if you'd want them to see you in your present state."

She rushed on up the stairs before her mother could knock her down them in her fearful rage and vituperations and frantically slammed the door on her and the foul language ensuing, locking it firmly.

The next day she noted with interest that her mother was up and about bright and early dressed for business and hastened on her way to the base. On her way out she unceremoniously dumped a carton in the hallway.

"Oh Fran, I brought some dolls for the kids, take what you think they'll like and I'll move the rest along."

Francis gaped, with the trouble she's in and it doesn't even faze her, she's completely unperturbed.

Olive flashed her daughter one of her famous smiles, "Fell off a lorry, Fran. Just know the girls will love them." With a wink, she was gone.

Curiosity getting the better of her, Francis pounced on the carton. She was flabbergasted at what she saw, beautiful dolls, so lifelike, decked out in gorgeous lace dresses; at least six boxes of them. Oh cripes better get these put away, she thought, don't want any more trouble. Wonder where she 'found' these.

Some days later, it was as Francis suspected, her mother said in passing, "Well it's their loss, Fran. They discharged me, can you believe that?"

Oh yes, I certainly can, her daughter thought privately but said nothing.

****

Belinda hurried down the street clutching her latest floral arrangement of wild flowers and natural greens in a basket. She had taken great pains with this preparation and gripped it tightly for fear of dropping it. Her face lit up as she rounded the corner and the little florist shop came into view. Over the previous months she had taken to studying the plant displays in the shop window and truly believing that she could do better had started putting her own presentations together. Finally on this day she plucked up the courage to cross over the threshold and into the shop. Once inside she was consumed with embarrassment when the owner of the store, Mrs. Graves appeared from the back regions. The older woman's first impression was that of surprise as she appraised the waiflike, pathetic little creature in her poor attire. There was no disputing the defensiveness in the girl's manner but Mrs. Graves' heart went out to her. Her little body was so fragile but her features clearly defined with huge sad dull eyes set in a delicately pale face surrounded by fair hair hanging straight bearing the semblance of a Page Boy style but very obviously cut by someone other than a professional. Belinda was very fair like her brother and sisters Maude and Davina and bore no resemblance to her two elder sisters Francis and Wanda who were of dark complexion with even darker eyes and an abundance of raven black hair.

Mrs. Graves noted the girl's delicate, artistically made hands and fingers surrounding her basket so beautifully arranged.

"Oh what a lovely arrangement, did you make that yourself?"

The girl's manner warmed immediately at the compliment and her eyes belied their sadness of a few moments previously by shining and brightening her entire face.

"Yes, Oh yes. I really did. I was hoping you would display it because I've been practising and thought I could make better displays than you have in your window." She rushed on her urgency increasing in her endeavour to sell herself.

"Well I would love to display your little basket and where do you think it should be placed?"

“What do you think of that?” the girl questioned having stepped up onto the window platform and very carefully placed her wild flowers.

“I’m very impressed that looks lovely. Let’s step outside and have a look from the street.”

The pair stood outside and stared. The older woman noted the look of awe on the girl’s face and sensed how important it was to her, obviously like a dream come true having her work admired and placed in the most strategic position of the entire window display. She took the girl’s arm and led her inside.

“Let’s discuss a little business over some tea and scones and decide how we can best help each other.”

She reached for her purse and pressed some coins into Belinda’s shaking hand.

“I didn’t come in here for money. I just thought I could make the window look better and I love making all sorts of arrangements.” Belinda was indignant; her guard was up and she tried to return the money.

“No”. Mrs. Graves retorted firmly and picking her words carefully, “I think you’ve designed an exquisite addition for the window and my mother always taught me to return a favour with another, so I insist you keep the money, you’ve earned it. Now let’s sit down and you can tell me about any other ideas you may have and how we can work things out together. I’d like to be friends and I can teach you all about the business as we go along. You can make displays and we can show and sell them. Don't you think that's a good idea?"

She laid the table and they sat down to scones with butter and jam and a lovely pot of tea with a knitted cosy covering the pot. This was to be the start of a new and better phase in both of their lives and of building a strong and everlasting friendship based on a deep-seated love and admiration for each other.

Promising to bring more arrangements, Belinda returned home that day filled with elation.

****

Francis sat quietly. Both daughters were having their afternoon nap and she revelled in the peace and contentment of the moment. Yes they should be tired, back in the woods again they were today with those gypsies. The two sisters could always be found up in the woods when the gypsies were back and had set up their camp. The younger child would avidly describe the music and dancing around the caravans and the horses in particular were always a fascination to both girls. Bedtime always brought a smile to Francis's face when she heard her elder daughter who was quite the story teller weaving a never ending saga about a rider named

Shenandoah and his horse and the adventures they both had. When she wanted to go to sleep her younger sister would always pester her for just one more story. These times were the deepest bonding of the two sisters, times which were treasured and never forgotten.

It was one of those rare times when the house was quiet and peaceful. Her quarters were on the top floor and although there were extreme inconveniences of getting too young children down three flights of stairs; she still preferred to be cut off from the rest of the household. It was too inconvenient for her mother to raid and steal her belongings; bad enough that she had managed to get Francis's wedding ring which had been carefully placed at the side of her bed after the second child was born. It was never located and Francis was never to wear any kind of ring again. Nobody really knew whether it was by choice or that she was so active and her hands always in the earth with her growing interest in gardening, exacerbating her obsession to scrub her hands raw.

Francis's thoughts drifted to the water meadows surrounding the town where she had spent many happy days laughing and joking and having swimming competitions with the village boys in the river. She was a strong swimmer and always gratified when she invariably beat them to the far bank; a dangerous sport considering the strength of the current in parts and they could easily have been swept away. That was all part of the fun and excitement of course. Francis smiled when she thought of it. Yes they had been her happiest moments and like her grandmother Martha, she loved the river and meadows with a passion.

Her pleasure at those times softened the reality of the rest of her life and what a life…

It hadn't been so bad in the early years for her but as her siblings grew, all of them, including herself, were ravaged with cold and hunger with no proper clothing and shoes falling off their feet. The shame of constant eviction and homeless for non-payment of rent coupled with the huge responsibility of having to look after her brother and sisters because her mother was never at home and her father worked away, made Francis cringe when she thought about it. What really haunted her was the horror of being deprived of even the basic cosmetic needs of a young girl entering womanhood and the shame of them all being sent home from school with bugs in their hair and nothing available to get rid of them.

Nevertheless, Francis made some allowance for her mother. Through no fault of her own, she was ostracized from the family and given away as a baby because of her mother's infidelity. Since her understanding of the magnitude of that rejection, she had closed her heart forever, the hurt buried deep within her. Her incapacity for empathy towards anybody least of all her own children was reflected in her treatment of everybody including her own children, which really was hard to forgive. Her first years were submerged in the First World War and then later the Second World War, along with her health being ruined by birthing one child after another; all served to have a negative influence on her; nevertheless, it was hard to accept the way their lives had been affected.

She recalled how Dugan came home on leave periodically to meet up with his sweetheart Elsie. They had known each other since childhood and had always been inseparable. The transition from friends to lovers was an easy switch as both adored the other. Elsie would listen for hours as Dugan would talk about how he was going to whisk her away to the United States, the land where dreams were spun into gold. How sad Francis thought, poor Dugan had returned on what he thought was his final trip to take Elsie back to the States as his bride. The money he had saved over many, many months to marry and take his new bride to a new life was gone. He had hidden it in his room for safekeeping but it disappeared. Francis always remembered vividly the bitter argument which ensued between Dugan and his mother. Years of hatred and bitterness came to the fore and Dugan had left, hardly saying goodbye. He worked his way back to the United States where he remained until he had saved another 'stake'.

Francis smiled when she thought of her brother and Elsie and her last sight of them. So happy were they, their faces radiant with love for each other, alive with excitement at the pending trip back to the United States. Dugan had managed to talk his way into a really good job with great prospects, guaranteeing a good start in the new country. It was an emotional experience for Francis as she said goodbye to her brother not knowing if she would ever see him again. He was to return a few times to his homeland but never wished to set eyes on his mother again. His hatred for her was all consuming and like Wanda carried with him for the rest of his life.

She remembered again when the war was over and evacuees such as Belinda and Davina had returned home from the country. What tales they had to tell; it must have been a couple of hours of non-stop talk, mostly about Nellie and her fabulous baking. The occasion of dinner was relayed with reverence, how everyone sat down as one big happy family. Francis chortled at the image of the pair of them saying grace and trying to refrain from grabbing the food and stuffing it back in their usual way. The girls relived the whole scene conveying every detail, from grace to the scrumptious home baked pies for desert so much so that they had Francis believing she had actually been there with them.

Nellie had been a real mother to them, caring and compassionate. She gave them a glimpse of a life they had never known. Memories they would hold dear forever. Francis wrinkled her nose when the girls talked about Rosie. Dear old Rosie how they grew to love that old mare and she obviously reciprocated. They told her how the horse always looked up and trotted eagerly across the pasture when she saw them coming to give her a daily carrot; another highlight of their day.

Francis was pleased for Davina and her closeness to Trevor who like Dugan had taken to the sea. He would 'lay off' in Southampton and come to the house laden with goodies for the girls, silk stockings, cosmetics, so many luxuries of which they had always been without. He always had special gifts for Davina.

The situation between Davina and her mother had been getting worse. The fierce arguments were turning to violence particularly when Olive had yet again stolen Davina's clothes. Both had terrible tempers and Francis was weary of physically separating them when they came to blows. Olive seemed to hate Davina almost as much as she hated Wanda. Francis assumed it was because of her sisters' obvious contempt for their mother. She shuddered as she remembered that last violent, terrible battle which had raged between her younger sister and mother. Davina had grabbed the bread knife and was brandishing it at her mother who had broken the lock on the door of Davina's room and taken her daughter's latest acquisitions bought by Trevor as gifts from abroad. Francis had intervened and taken the knife away from her sister, running the risk of serious injury in the scuffle. Olive had gone blazing out of the house screaming at Davina to be gone when she got back. Fortunately, Trevor was back in town and when he burst through the door was horrified as Francis relayed to him the latest escapade.

"I've put Davina in my room but she'll have to go. One of them is going to kill the other, it's not safe anymore."

"Don't fret yourself any more. You've done more than your share of taking care of everybody. You've got enough to do. I'll take her back to Dorset with me. Mum will look after her and when she's old enough I'll marry her. I'll always look after her. As long as I'm around she'll be all right."

Trevor was as good as his word. He loved and protected Davina throughout his days.

Well that just leaves Belinda and Maude, thought Francis. She still took care of her sisters in their parents' absence which was pretty much all the time. Following the war her father had signed on in the Merchant Navy as a carpenter. When Victor signed off his ship, there was the usual round of pubbing for him and Olive until their money ran out, then Olive would pursue him until he got another ship's contract. His life was a misery until he took to sea again.

She had always been very concerned about Belinda who suffered severe nervous disorders and insecurities obviously resulting from a violent and confrontational environment and fear of her mother and their hand-to-hand way of living. Her childlike innocence and fascination for all living organisms and natural floribunda was heart-warming. Her skills at collecting and assembling various plants had developed into designing wonderful floral arrangements in baskets or pots, whatever she could get hold of. She had been spending every available moment in the local flower shop studying their displays. Mrs. Graves was her mentor and was so impressed with the girl's great sense of artistry that she befriended her, always ensuring that she had the necessary items of toiletry and other much needed items for a growing girl. Belinda spent every waking moment at the shop learning the trade and the lady was only too happy to teach her everything she knew about the business.

Francis was overjoyed when Mrs. Graves, who had nurtured a growing affection over the months, asked if Belinda could occupy the spare room above the shop. She was aware of the girl's plight at home and the situation with her mother and wished to take her under her wing and give her a chance at life which had so far eluded the young woman. She assured Francis that Belinda was great company and very good in the shop. Francis knew that Belinda's level of nervous anxiety and hypertension was always lowered when she was away from her mother and the house and was in the process of making the arrangements for Belinda to go. She knew only too well that she'd get no argument from her mother on that score. Mrs. Graves was going to see that Belinda received her board and food in exchange for help in the shop and some light housekeeping. The girl would get the opportunity to learn the trade and receive a small remuneration as well. Francis was ecstatic as she thought about the situation. Belinda would be living in clean conditions, learning a trade and earning a small allowance to get her clothing, etc., up together. What a stroke of luck.

Then there was Maude. Maude's boyfriend, like Trevor, took good care of his beau. Francis thought about Jeff and remembered what fun they all had together. Even though she was now married in a very different situation, with children, they still all had great gatherings together and enjoyed each other's company immensely. Times were tough but they had all been there for each other, Dugan and Elsie, Davina and Trevor, Maude and Jeff. All the boys had ended up at sea. Jeff had plans also to go to the United States. He was qualified in welding and heavy-duty equipment maintenance and was ambitious to 'move up the ladder'. He was bent on establishing good contacts in the United States. He wanted to work in a brand new country that was offering so many opportunities for young people who would put down roots and start a new life and family.

His parents, although rough, had taken Maude in on many occasions to escape her mother's abuse and when things got to be intolerable at home. Francis had no qualms about Maude following Jeff back to his family. They had plans to get married and his family wanted to take her in as part of their group.

Francis marvelled at how Wanda and Leo were still so very happy together. Wanda was a difficult girl so determined to better herself becoming fiercely competitive striving for more and more material goods, determining to be better than everybody else, commendable up to a point but Wanda's obsessions with aesthetics had the potential to be damaging to her and her future family which proved to be the case through the course of time. She could be totally overbearing at times and never gave up trying to outrun her past. Leo's mother had been as good as her word and provided a decent home for the girl. The couple intended on immigrating to Australia when they had saved a bit of a nest egg. Even though it was on the other side of the world, Wanda always said there weren't enough miles to separate them from her mother.

Well, it looks like we've made it against all odds, Francis thought heaving a huge sigh of relief. Unwittingly our mother made us strong. In spite of her and everything going against us, we've survived, literally clawing our way from hell to a future with people who care about us. Somebody up there must have been looking out for us after all.

Francis's own life was still harsh with two children to raise, but Davina and Belinda were about to start new phases in their lives which would definitely lighten the load. Her disposition was bright as she sat on that day watching the sun slant into the horizon. Hamish entered her thoughts as a sudden breath of fresh air. Dear gentle Hamish, doing his best, loving her so deeply. How lucky she was. He was sparing no effort in researching ear specialists who could possibly help with her hearing problem and increasing deafness. It was so difficult as they all seemed to be based in London operating out of the Middlesex Hospital but he was determined that she would receive a full medical analysis.

Hamish generally had a book in his pocket and was always spouting poetry to her initially causing her much embarrassment. Gradually he opened her mind to good literature and she became a determined student, anxious to keep up with her new husband and fiercely trying to build some confidence and abate the sense of inferiority she had always felt because of her lack of education. Her sense of inadequacy and insecurity was never completely dispelled throughout her lifetime even though she never ceased striving to better herself in every way both educationally and in her personal appearance appropriate to the position of RAF Service Wife of which she was very proud.

So that just leaves the two girls and me. What's going to happen with us? Francis thought. We have to get out of here soon. She had never wanted to get involved with the service accommodation or the life in service quarters it offered, but Hamish was firmly established in a career in the RAF which now provided living accommodation for service families. She was getting used to the idea of living as a service wife. At least she'd have a secure roof and maybe, just maybe if she and Hamish saved really hard, they might one day have their own house with a garden and maybe even a dog. Yes the girls would like a dog and we'd be a real family. Francis closed her eyes and savoured the thought, her very own home, a clean home with plenty of fresh clean linen and lots and lots of soap and her own garden. Her spirit rallied; her mood sanguine and hope filled her heart. Rousing herself, she moved forward purposefully to prepare for the evening meal.

Epilogue

Martha & Roman

They were found in tight embrace on the banks of the river. Separated in life; their choice to be together in death. Both souls finally at peace carried by the wind to their infinity setting them free forever. It is said that, on occasion, a sharp ear can pick up the sounds of lilting laughter and the lyrics of a gypsy love song blending with the trill of the birds and the cleansing wash of the chalk streams wending down to the sea.

Lyza

Her grave unvisited and untended nevertheless beautiful, abounding with wild flowers almost obliterating the stark surround. Her headstone bears only her name, birth

date and the year of her demise; forgotten by all except one; a little girl who had waited so patiently for the taxi to take her auntie to heaven. Who, throughout her life and troubled times would hold a little prayer book presented to Lyza in 1883; look for the brightest star in the sky and remember the words of an old lady she had known for such a short time, but, nevertheless, loved so dearly.

Olive

A piano sounds in the seedy side of town and a heavenly voice rings out the strains of a sentimental love song. The air is charged with emotion and the crowd, bar none are moved to tears at the pure sweet voice of Olive, the voice of an angel … or so they say!